THE PURGATORIUM

THE PURGATORIUM, BOOK ONE

Eva Pohler

Eva Pohler Books
20011 Park Ranch
San Antonio, Texas 78259
www.evapohler.com

Book Layout ©2017 BookDesignTemplates.com

Book Cover Design by Wydawnictwo Replika

The Purgatorium/ Eva Pohler. -- 1st ed.
Paperback ISBN: 978-1-958390-51-1

Are you one of the living or the dead?

—A GHOST

Contents

For my family.

The Island

A morning fog was just beginning to thin in the sticky, ocean breeze. Whether it was the sharp smell of dead fish or lingering anxiety from the plane ride, Daphne could not eat when Cam offered to buy her a snack at a stand in the harbor. He bought himself a baked pretzel, and then the two of them followed Dr. Hortense Gray up the ramp and onto the catamaran, pulling their bags behind them.

They maneuvered through a crowd of school-age children in matching yellow t-shirts. Of the twenty or so other passengers, most were men in their thirties and forties. She and Cam were the only teenagers aboard.

Daphne stood at the railing overlooking the water with Cam on one side of her and the doctor on the other. The wind whipped her brown hair around her face despite her efforts to tuck it behind her ears. She missed this beauty. She'd forgotten how breathtaking it was. Her parents used to take her and her brother and sister to the beach all the time. There was nothing like gazing at the ocean where it met the sky on the horizon.

But the beauty could not stop her from trembling, could not stop the dread gripping her chest. Cam had said a wildlife refuge and a resort with pristine beaches. He hadn't said a thing about therapeutic exercises. She'd had to hear it from this strange doctor who had met them at the airport in Ventura. Was the doctor like a life coach? Would Daphne have to climb a rock wall or plunge down a zipline? She should have known her parents wouldn't let her go with Cam to a getaway resort just for fun. She should have been more suspicious. Tears pricked her eyes. She felt betrayed. Betrayed by her parents and her best friend.

As the catamaran reached the open sea, a pod of dolphins leapt ahead of them, as if guiding them to their destination.

"Look!" Cam pointed at the group of four leaping in turns from the water beside the boat.

Daphne's cheeks stretched into a smile in spite of everything. The dolphins were amazing.

"Just wait," Cam said, his blond hair flattening against his head with the wind. "We might see a humpback whale. Keep your fingers crossed."

She stood close to Cam's tall, wiry frame as though the two years they had rarely spoken had never existed. She hadn't even so much as texted him a happy birthday wish last month when he had turned eighteen. For the millionth time, she wished she could go back to that night she had failed to get out of bed.

An hour passed with no humpback sightings, but soon a great mound of rock could be seen—bald, solid, smooth like the skin of a whale, and round like a bowling ball. Daphne couldn't imagine how such a rocky place could hold any kind of paradise. Then a long, narrow pier became visible, and beside it, a rocky beach. The boat docked at the end of the pier, and all but Daphne, Cam, the doctor, and the captain climbed out.

Where were the pristine beaches?

The captain then turned the boat north and skirted around to another part of the island, where there were more rocky crags with waves crashing into and away from them, tossing the boat side to side, until they came into a large harbor full of other boats.

To Daphne's right were hundreds of pelicans roosting on a rocky beach of shale. Some slept standing up, others cleaned their feathers, and still others walked around inspecting the shoreline and the shallow waters surrounding it.

Kara would have liked this, she thought.

"They're looking for sardines in the kelp beds," Cam said.

Daphne used her hand as a visor. "Look at them all."

An even longer pier than the first shot out into the harbor, and they were now moving to it.

"Prisoners Harbor," Cam said.

This side of the island was certainly more beautiful than the eastern point at Scorpion Anchorage, but Daphne still saw no evidence of pristine beaches. A wildlife refuge this island may be, but where was the resort?

Once they docked, Daphne and Cam followed Dr. Gray up five rungs on a ladder to the pier, and then they dragged their luggage across the narrow row of boards toward several flights of steps. Descending from the steps ahead of them were two people, an African-American boy and girl in their teens. The girl was bald as the rock at Scorpion Anchorage, as though she had undergone chemotherapy.

"Look at me!" the girl growled at Dr. Gray, and Daphne thought perhaps they were related, having the same round dark eyes and high cheek bones.

"Come along, Daphne," Dr. Gray said, ignoring the girl.

The girl grabbed Daphne's wrist and started to say something, but Cam moved between them.

"We don't want any trouble," he said.

"Are you okay?" Daphne asked the girl, trying to see around Cam, but the bald teen turned away, scuttled down the pier, and quickly boarded the boat.

"What's her deal?" Daphne asked Cam.

"Don't know," he said, leading her onward.

"That was odd."

"Yeah. It was. Come on."

The squawking of the pelicans could be heard from the several flights of wooden steps, but they were less visible until Daphne reached the summit near a dirt road, where a jeep and its driver waited. The driver was an older man, maybe in his forties, with tanned skin and a straw cowboy hat. He nodded at them as they approached.

"Hello, Roger," Dr. Gray said.

"Nice to have you back, Hortense," the driver said with a southern drawl. "The island ain't the same without you."

From this point, Daphne looked out over the ocean and, although the view was spectacular, she frowned. This wasn't what she had expected.

It wasn't like she hadn't asked a lot of questions. Cam had gone the summer before, and then, this summer, one rare evening while she'd sat in her tree in the backyard, the thick oak leaves forming a shield around her, he had told her about it.

She hadn't seen him in the treehouse on the other side of the six-foot wooden fence that separated their two yards. When he called out to her, she'd been crying again, and although she had wanted to scramble down the trunk and run inside and hide, he'd asked her a question that had made her pause.

"If you could spend your final days anywhere in the whole wide world, where would it be?"

"Are you drunk?" she had asked.

"No. Just curious. " Then he had added, "I miss you, Daph."

"I'd spend my last days on a beach somewhere beautiful," she had said.

"I know just the place." He had jumped from his treehouse, had bolted over the fence, and had landed at the base of her tree faster than she had been able to wipe her eyes.

"I'm sorry you didn't get to see a humpback," Cam said beside her now. "Maybe on the way back."

They drove by picnic tables, trees, a kayak rental, and an outhouse as the driver took them along a canyon ridge toward the center of the island. A few minutes later they came up on two other buildings with solar panels turned toward the sun, a long wooden deck, and two greenhouses. To their right was a deeper valley with a stream running down the middle and pine trees.

"Look there!" Hortense Gray pointed above the valley. "A bald eagle. See it?"

"Oh, yeah," Daphne said.

"Isn't it fantastic?" Cam handed her a pair of binoculars from his bag. "Use these."

She took them and looked closely at the majestic bird as it soared through the sky above the valley.

"See if you can spot any foxes," Cam said, full of enthusiasm.

Daphne scoured the landscape for wildlife. Gulls flew to and from the sea up high above where the eagle soared. The valley looked like a manicured fairway on a top-notch golf course with a stream running down the middle of it and branching off into smaller ones. Along the sides of the "fairway" were pines and shrubs and grassy knolls. The spring ran heavily from the highland but narrowed in places where it gently rushed over rocks.

A figure stepped into her view through the binoculars, but it was no fox. She watched it, focused the lenses. It was a person. A hiker? A girl with long black hair trailing behind her ran along the stream, turning back to look, as though she were being followed.

Just then a man grabbed the girl by the hair and dragged her back up the hill and into a copse of trees.

Daphne's stomach dropped. "Oh my God!"

"What?" Dr. Gray asked.

Daphne's tongue twisted in her mouth as she stammered, "A man….and a girl! He's hurting her!"

The doctor took the binoculars and pointed them toward the valley. "Where? I don't see anything?"

"I swear they're out there," Daphne said, her stomach forming a knot. "I saw them. We have to do something!" She gave Cam a pleading look, and said again, "We have to do something." Why wasn't he more alarmed? "We have to go down there and help her. What are we waiting for?"

"Roger, take us down into the valley, please," Dr. Gray said.

The driver sped downhill. The road ended about twenty yards from the spring. Roger stopped the jeep, and all four climbed out.

Daphne pointed to the ground, insistently. "They were here, I swear I saw them. He was pulling her by the hair."

When the adults looked back at her blankly, she took off running through the nearby trees, her heart beating wildly. Why wasn't anyone taking her seriously? Panic had overtaken her, and she couldn't think. She couldn't think. "Hello?" She saw and heard no one.

The others also called out and began to search the trees.

After several minutes, they all met up again.

Dr. Gray said, "Oh, this is no good."

"What should we do?" Cam asked, out of breath.

The doctor put a hand on Daphne's shoulder. "Please don't be offended by what I'm about to say."

Daphne couldn't believe the patronizing look on the taller woman's face. "I didn't imagine it," she said, panting.

"It's been a long, tiring trip, and islands are famous for their mirages, especially this one," Dr. Gray said.

"Not mirages," Roger said. "Ghosts."

"Please, Roger. Don't start." Dr. Gray shook her head.

"What ghosts?" Daphne asked. Even though she didn't believe in ghosts, goosebumps popped up along her arms.

"Let's go on to the resort," Dr. Gray said. "I'll phone the naval guards when we get there and tell them what you saw."

"What ghosts?" Daphne asked again in the jeep in the backseat beside Cam. She twisted back with her eyes held up to the binoculars, scanning the stream and nearby woods for signs of the girl and her attacker as the jeep climbed toward the canyon ridge.

"We aren't going to talk about nonsense," the doctor said.

"She has a right to know about the island's legends," Roger objected.

"Is this the one about Misink?" Cam asked. "The guy who threw the men in the ocean and took the women on his rainbow bridge?"

Hortense Gray turned from the front passenger seat. "The Chumash believed the first people grew from seeds planted on this island by the Earth Goddess, Hutash. When the island became overpopulated with people, she sent down Misink, the guardian of nature, to set things right. They say each year Misink threw six young men into the ocean where they turned into dolphins. That's why the Chumash consider the dolphins to be their brothers.

"Misink also took six unmarried women and had them for himself. They say he took them into the sky by way of his rainbow bridge, and they were never seen alive again."

"What does this have to do with ghosts?" Daphne put down the binoculars, the deep valley now out of view.

Roger said, "People say Misink comes for women about your age to take with him to the skies, and sometimes they come back and wander this here island."

"Interesting legend, but you don't expect me to believe that was Misink out there in the valley, do you?" Daphne smelled a set-up. "Is this some kind of joke?" She expected one of them to say, *Bwahahahaha*, any minute now.

Roger coughed and cleared his voice.

Cam whispered, "Apparently Roger is a believer."

"Like you can talk," she whispered back. Cam had made plenty of claims throughout their childhood of having seen his grandmother in his attic. Her brother, Joey, a year older than Cam, still believed Cam's grandmother spoke to him.

Roger said, "I dare you to spend one night at the old Christy Ranch, and then you can laugh at me all you like."

"What's old Christy Ranch?" Daphne asked.

"It's on the western end of the island," Roger said. "That there ranch house is haunted by the wife of a slave trader."

"Have you seen her ghost?" Cam asked.

"No, but I've heard the screaming."

"What screaming?" Daphne asked.

"Out on Haunted Bridge," Roger replied. "I've heard the screaming with my own ears. My pal and I searched all over in the morning and found no trace of anyone and no explanation for the screams. People say the wife of the slave trader was horrified when she learned what her husband done, and, once when he was headed back for more slaves, she sunk his ship with him and his crew aboard. They say she went crazy until she died. They say she's responsible for a lot of the ships that wreck in that there part of the sea."

As they made their descent into the canyon, no one said more about the incident Daphne may or may not have seen. Daphne was tired and had eaten little. Maybe she *had* imagined the figures in the valley.

Joey, her brother, saw people who weren't there all the time. Daphne worried one day she would begin to see them, too.

No. She knew what she had seen. They'd been real, flesh and blood, living people. But something gave her the feeling that Dr. Gray and Roger were messing with her.

CHAPTER TWO

A New Friend

As the jeep topped the ridge, the resort came into view at the bottom of the canyon. It consisted of a swimming pool, tennis courts, and a large central building surrounded by fifty or so smaller, single cabanas, which reminded Daphne of Tiki huts.

The jeep pulled up to the cabana marked with the number one on a bamboo post. Hortense Gray climbed out and crossed onto the patio in front of the unit, where there were two rockers and a table. So far so good. The bright red door where the doctor stooped with a key was flanked by two windows. The wind was milder down here in the canyon. Roger carried in Daphne's bags behind Dr. Gray and then returned to the jeep. Daphne and Cam followed the doctor inside.

The unit was small but nicely decorated, cool, and comfortable. To the left was a queen bed with a rich red duvet that seemed to invite Daphne to crawl beneath it and rest. To the right were two upholstered chairs in stripes of red and gold with a coffee table in front of them. Perfect reading chairs, she thought. (She had brought along two books that had always been on her bucket list: *Gone with the Wind* and *To Kill a Mockingbird*.) Straight ahead, was a wooden armoire, and above it was a painting of Hercules slaying the Hydra.

A bit intense, but whatever.

"Do you have any questions before we leave you to settle in?" Dr. Gray asked.

"Do we get Wifi out here?"

"No, not yet," the doctor replied.

"Cell reception?"

"Sorry."

"Television?"

Dr. Gray smiled. "Yes. That we do have. I believe there are forty-one channels."

At least there was some connection to civilization, Daphne thought.

"Oh, one more thing," Daphne said, and Hortense Gray turned from the door to look at her again. "When do those therapeutic games you mentioned begin?"

"Soon, dear."

Before Daphne could ask more about them, the doctor added, "Now make yourself at home. I'll see you at dinner." With that, the doctor left the room.

Daphne looked at Cam with narrowed eyes, but he kissed her cheek and said, "I'll be right back. Just going to unpack."

As upset as Daphne felt over Cam springing this surprise therapy on her, she hoped to carry out her plan within the next couple of days. She went to the kitchenette to open the drawers. Yes, there were knives. She hadn't seen kitchen knives in months. She took one from the drawer and brought it closer to her eyes, running a finger along the blade. When the time was right, this would do.

When she returned the blade to its drawer, the hair on the back of her neck prickled as she heard someone whisper her name. "Daphne."

She looked around the kitchen and the other rooms and saw no one. What the heck? She knew she was tired from the plane and boat rides and still freaked out about what had happened in the valley, and the wind was blowing a palm against her room. Maybe it was only the wind she had heard.

After she found her bikini and purple bathing suit cover and dug out her small case so she could brush her teeth and comb her hair, the doorbell rang.

"That was fast," she said, opening the door, but the guy standing on the other side was not Cam.

"Oh," she said, stuffing her hands into her bathing suit cover pockets. "Sorry, I was expecting someone else." She felt the blood rush to her cheeks.

The man grinned. He was taller than Cam and handsome, tan and nicely built, maybe mid-twenties, with golden brown eyes and dark curly hair on his head and bare chest. He had a cleft in his chin and dimples when he smiled. He wore swim trunks and sandals and a towel across one shoulder.

"Can I help you?" Daphne asked.

"I'm behind you in Unit Two and wanted to introduce myself. I'm Stan."

Daphne fished her hand out of her pocket and awkwardly took his. "Nice to meet you. I'm Daphne."

"Hey, Stan, how's it going?" Cam walked up to the door. "Looks like you've met Daph. I was just going to show her the beach."

"I was heading over myself. I'll catch you there."

"See you in a bit, then."

"See you," Daphne said.

Cam came in and Daphne closed the door. She looked him over. She hadn't seen him in a bathing suit in years, and he'd filled out nicely.

"Wow," he said, giving her a once over. "You look hotter than the twin suns of Tatooine."

A sharp laugh rose from her throat. "Oh, God. I'd thought I'd heard the last of your *Star Wars* jokes."

"Glad to see I haven't lost my touch," he said. "It still makes you laugh like a little girl."

"You must have missed my eye rolling. Let me do it for you once more." She rolled her eyes with exaggeration.

"So what do you think of the place so far?" he asked.

"You mean except for the girl who might be dead in the valley?"

His face sobered. "The naval guards are looking into it. We did what we could."

"You don't seem too upset about it. You do believe me, don't you? Or do you think I imagined it?"

"I believe you." He squeezed her shoulders, making her heart hammer against her ribs. "But we did what we could."

She slipped on a pair of flip-flops and followed him from the room.

"Do you think Dr. Gray and Roger were messing with us?" she asked.

Cam kicked a stone from the sidewalk. "What do you mean?"

"What happened in the valley was just so odd, you know? Like a set-up."

"But why would they do that?"

"You tell me."

They walked down the sidewalk, past the pool, where a few sun-bathers lounged on the deck, and past the main building, where others were going in and out, and continued toward a steep cliff edge of the canyon. Built along the cliff edge were several flights of wooden steps, like the ones they climbed from the pier at Prisoners Harbor.

"More steps," she said.

"I promise it's worth it."

As they reached the summit, the wind blew Daphne's hair every which way, so she pulled it back into a ponytail, using the band she wore on her wrist.

"It's beautiful," she said, looking out over the sea.

The beach below was indeed pristine, with soft white sand along the shoreline, foamy waves gently lapping up and back, gulls flying over-head, and as they made their way down a few more steps to a board-walk, she couldn't stop saying, "It's so beautiful."

There were no boats in the U-shaped cove. To their left was an end-less hill of yellow poppies rising up toward the horizon, and to their right, chalky bluffs spotted with sparse mounds of grass. Below were the white sandy beach and the bluest water Daphne had ever seen. The waves were gentle, inviting. Sitting on the sand with his feet in the water, sandals and towel beside him, was Stan, throwing a stone into the sea. There were no other people around.

When they reached him, Stan said, "There you are. I was about to go in without you."

Daphne took off her flip-flops and stood where the water reached her feet. "It's so cold! Oh my crap, that's cold!" She stepped away.

"It's refreshing," Stan said.

"Exhilarating," Cam added. "I'm going in."

Cam ran into the sea. Soon, he was far out and in deep to his chest, jumping up and down like a big ape, beckoning her in.

"He's crazy," Daphne said. "I think I'll just bathe in the sun awhile." She pulled off her cover and sat in her bikini in the sand beside Stan.

He climbed to his feet and said, "Oh, no. You're not getting away with that." He picked her up in his arms, despite her screams of protest, and carried her into the water.

"Stop! This is freezing!" She found herself hoping he wouldn't put her down. His arms, his chest, his chin and mouth so near hers, were intoxicating. "Eeeh!" she squealed.

Cam swam over to them, glistening in the sun with the water dripping down his hair, face, and shoulders. He looked like a golden god. "Hey! Give her back!"

Cam reached out for her, and every part of her skin touched by the two guys broke out in goose bumps. She was sandwiched between them and hyper-aware of their skin on hers when Cam ripped her from Stan's arms, lifted her, and tossed her into the icy water.

She was laughing hysterically when she popped back up. She couldn't recall the last time she'd laughed. *Really* laughed. Interacting with people wasn't something she did much anymore, but this was okay, wasn't it? Kara wouldn't begrudge her one last hurrah before Daphne joined her in the afterlife.

Before thoughts of Kara sobered her, she pushed them down and returned her focus to the boys. Stan splashed her, laughing, and then swam away. Cam picked her up and heaved her in the water, and when she resurfaced, his legs were pointing to the sky, making her laugh again. They used to do handstands in her backyard pool with Joey and Kara, and they'd make her mother judge. Her mother would sit on the white wrought iron chair in the shade with a book in her hand and her frosted hair pulled back in the headband she still wore every day of her life. Now, Daphne went down and pressed her hands against the cold sand, wobbling a bit as she worked to keep her legs together and point her toes. Before she'd mastered her form, she could feel Cam tickling the bottoms of her feet, and she was awash with childhood memories. Happy ones. She came up laughing.

Then she climbed onto Cam's shoulders like she used to for chicken fights, back when it was always Joey and Kara against her and Cam. Then Cam fell back and pulled her under with him. The joy surged through her. She was elated that her final days would be happy ones. Nothing mattered anymore. Nothing at all. There was just this moment, right now, and nothing else. No horrible past, no dreadful future. She felt free.

They played for a while longer before Cam challenged her to a race back to shore, which he won.

"If we were swimming, I'd 've won hands down!" she said.

"That's why it was a foot race," he said. He took her hand. "Come on."

They walked along the beach to the bluffs and back and then stretched out on the warm sand beneath the sun to dry. Daphne lay on her stomach on top of her swim cover. Stan later came and joined them, lying on his back beside Daphne, breathing heavily from his swim. She watched the rise and fall of his chest until it slowed down to normal. Then she closed her eyes.

As nice as it felt lying between these two gorgeous guys, Daphne missed Brock. He was as tall as Stan but thicker, with hair as dark as his, but not as curly, and he had the bluest eyes. His lips were soft, pouty, and thick. They were luscious when they swept across hers and really sweet when he smiled.

She turned over to watch the gulls and the waves, trying to forget.

On their way back, the three of them went to the main building and played a game of pool. Daphne played on both teams, since she wasn't that good, until she and Stan won and gloated over Cam with their high fives. Then Stan left to rest before dinner, and she and Cam played ping pong until two guys and a girl about their age came in to play billiards. Cam briefly introduced them, and then she and Cam decided to check out the pool.

It was an Olympic-size pool. At one end, it formed an "L" where it bent to a deeper end with a diving board and water slide. A hundred or so white loungers and chairs with tables were lined up along the deck, straight and orderly. Only two were occupied by sun-bathers. The water in the pool was clean and, presently, empty.

Cam took Daphne's hand and led her to the edge of the pool, gently at first, and then with force.

"What are you up to?" she asked.

"Trust me." He pulled her into his arms and tumbled the both of them over the edge.

When she opened her eyes, she couldn't believe what she saw below her: a glass bottom revealing a sea cave with dozens of colorful fish and coral. Daphne swam up for a breath and then dove back down, overwhelmed by the beauty and the novelty of this aquarium-like pool. Cam took her hand and pointed at a moray eel wedged in the wall of the cave. Sea urchins waved their colorful tendrils as they fed from a bed of kelp. Daphne felt incredibly happy and in awe of this amazing place as she and Cam each took another breath and submerged, hand in hand and gazing at the sea-life beneath them. They resurfaced and returned to the pool edge, holding on to the stone deck while their bodies dangled in the water.

"It's incredible." She gulped air and dove down for one more look. Then she joined Cam on the deck loungers to dry in the sun.

She turned to study him while his eyes were closed. Although he had filled out, she could still see the little boy that had been her friend for so long. She missed those days when her brother and sister and Cam and she shared carefree days together. Tears threatened to run down her cheeks, and before she could bat them away, Cam opened his eyes and saw her looking at him.

"You okay?"

She giggled and sniffed. "Just overwhelmed." She couldn't tell him the whole truth—about the immense relief she felt over the fact that she would never have to face her parents' disappointed faces again. No more past. No more future. It was liberating. "This whole place is amazing. Thank you for telling me about it. I can't believe my parents let me come."

"You're welcome." He gave her a sweet smile. "I'm glad you're here."

She felt mixed emotions threatening to wash over her, and she didn't want to cry, so she asked, "So what's the scoop on Stan?"

"He's been here a few weeks now, I think. Came from Arizona. He goes to a university there. Studies history and anthropology, I think. Why, do you like him?"

She stood up and punched his arm. "Oh, shut up! Come on." She pulled him from the lounger. "Take me back to my room so I can get ready for dinner." As they walked along the sidewalk, hand in hand, she asked, "So when do the therapeutic games begin?"

"How do you know they haven't already?"

She squinted. "What's that supposed to mean?" Was the incident in the valley a game?

"Nothing." He looked down at his feet.

As they continued on to her unit, he said, "Just remember, no matter what happens here, no matter what you may think later, this is a good place."

"Cam, you're scaring me."

He sighed. "I'm trying to do the exact opposite. I'm asking you to trust me."

CHAPTER THREE

The Games

That evening, after a quick shower, Daphne dried her hair and lounged in her towel, waiting for Cam to call. While she waited, she opened her journal to add more lines to her new poem:

Since your voice can never be heard again,
Nor your touch felt, nor your eyes seen,
I'll close my eyes, and with one long sigh,
Seek you in my final dream.

Not long after, Cam phoned to say he would meet Daphne in the dining room because he'd promised Hortense he'd help set up an exercise.

"What kind of exercise?"

"Now how much fun would it be if I ruined the surprise?"

"I don't like surprises."

"Well, you're no fun. Come on, have a positive attitude. It's going to be great."

She hung up the phone and then put on a soft cream blouse with a long lavender skirt and silver sandals, a new outfit her mother had bought her for the trip. Daphne looked at her reflection as she twisted her hair up into a clip. She hadn't worn makeup or jewelry in a long time, but tonight, she wished she had brought some along.

A few others entered the main building way ahead of her. Behind her, Stan called for her to wait up. She turned and gasped. In a button-down, light-blue shirt and khakis, he looked every bit the male model.

"Hey," she said.

"Hey. You look nice."

"Thanks. So do you."

They followed the others into the main building.

"This place is so beautiful," Daphne said.

"Yeah. I've really enjoyed it here."

"How long are you staying?"

"Not sure. Kind of playing it by ear."

People stood in front of the elevator waiting. Daphne's palms felt sweaty. It had been a while since she had last been in one.

"Do you mind if we take the stairs?" Daphne asked at the last second, just as the doors opened to welcome them inside.

"Not at all."

She followed Stan down the hall, but the door to the stairwell had a sign posted: "Wet paint. Do not enter."

"Is there another stairwell?" Daphne asked. Her heart was racing now.

"I would think so. Come on." He led her down another corridor. They passed the rec room, the spa, the bar and grill, and came to the shop. "Here we go." But on the door was the same message. "Oops. Looks like the elevator it is."

They returned to the lobby and found one waiting. Daphne stepped inside with wobbly legs. As the elevator doors closed, Stan pushed number three, and Daphne's heart pounded all the way up in her ears. She clutched the railing behind her and looked for her happy place, chastising herself for going so long without riding an elevator. Her doctor had warned her that the desensitizing therapy would wear off. *Breathe in, two, three, four, and out, six, seven, eight.*

The doors opened on the third floor.

He led her through a foyer into the dining room. Daphne took another deep breath and slowly exhaled.

About a dozen tables were occupied, and a dozen more were not. Daphne spotted Cam across the room standing near a round table where Hortense and a few others in their forties and fifties were seated.

"You look great," Cam said, meeting her halfway.

"Thanks. So do you." She liked his gray shirt and black trousers and how they brought out the gold in his blue eyes and the highlights in his blond hair, a nice distraction from her nerves.

Stan followed them to the table, which was topped with glasses of iced tea and water and plates of salad and rolls.

"We're sitting over there," Cam pointed to another round table filled with younger people, in their teens and twenties. "But first I want to introduce you to a few others."

They said hello to Hortense Gray, and then Cam introduced Daphne to Arturo Gomez, the owner of the resort. He was short and had small hands. On each finger, he wore a ring with a big stone. He also wore a black tuxedo with a flamboyant turquoise bowtie and matching vest. His hair was slicked back, and his mustache lay across his upper lip like an asp. He seemed nice enough, but there was something about him that Daphne did not trust—an eagerness or enthusiasm that seemed out of place. He asked Daphne if she was enjoying her stay so far, and she said absolutely, telling him how much she loved the glass bottom pool and the private beach.

"There's much more to experience," he said with a Spanish accent. "I hope you like every bit of it."

Another man sat at Dr. Gray's left. Cam introduced him as Dr. Lee Reynolds, Dr. Gray's colleague in behavioral psychology. He was tall, thin, and bald, and appeared to be in his fifties or sixties. His head towered above everyone else's at the table even though he sat with his shoulders hunched over, like his body was too hard for him to hold upright. He said hello in a soft, effeminate voice, and although he was polite, he, too, gave Daphne a strange feeling, as though there were more to him than met the eye.

An older woman in her late fifties with curly white hair sat beside Lee Reynolds and was introduced as Mary Ellen Jones. She had round, chipmunk cheeks and an equally round body, and when she smiled, she made Daphne think of Mrs. Santa Claus. Roger, the driver, was also with them, along with a redhead in her late thirties named Kelly something, and a Native American man in his forties whose name Daphne did not hear (and she was too shy to ask to have it repeated). After these introductions, Cam and Stan led her to the table where the younger crowd was seated.

Although they all told Daphne their names, she couldn't remember them after having learned so many at the other table. There was a girl with long brown hair and green eyes, a Hispanic boy who looked college-age, and a thin blond boy who didn't talk much but smiled a lot. She recognized them as the group who had come to play billiards earlier.

Throughout the meal, they made small talk. Daphne mentioned her interest in the kayaking and horseback riding excursions, and both Stan and Cam said they wanted to join her. Cam encouraged her to go on the bird hiking trail, ranting about the island scrub jay and its near-extinction and how this island was the only place in the world you could see one. Stan told her she must do the island fox hunt—the creatures were fascinating, more like terriers than foxes, and you don't actually shoot them, just spot them.

During dessert, Daphne noticed Mr. Gomez being summoned by one of the waiters. After some time, he returned, white-faced, to the microphone near the stage.

"I hope everyone is enjoying their stay here at the Santa Cruz Island Resort." Mr. Gomez paused as everyone applauded. "Wonderful. Unfortunately I have troubling news. The dead body of a young woman was discovered in the valley this evening." A gasp traveled through the room. "The authorities believe she was murdered." People turned to one another with looks of alarm. "Don't be afraid. I have four more security guards coming in from the mainland, and they'll arrive tonight. I only tell you this news so you will take extra precautions. Use common sense. Don't go anywhere alone. Stay near the resort at night. The navy guards and employees of the Nature Conservancy are searching the grounds for the culprit. It's likely he is already gone from the island. Just be careful."

Daphne wanted to say, "So it wasn't a mirage, or ghosts," but she bit her lip because there was something strange about the whole situation that didn't sit right with her. She couldn't put her finger on it, but it seemed to her that they were all actors putting on a show. Mr. Gomez reminded her of Dumbledore when he tells the students at Hogwarts that there are places in the castle that are off limits. Nothing seemed authentic. But that made no sense. A whole ballroom full of people couldn't possibly be acting.

She told Cam she wanted to go back to her room. He said he had to help Dr. Gray first and would meet her there shortly.

She glanced across the room and then leaned closer to Cam. "But I'm really upset." Whether it *was* all a ruse, or a girl really had been murdered, either scenario had sucked away the feelings of liberty that had been making Daphne unusually happy.

"I'll walk you back," Stan offered.

She waited for Cam to say, "No, that's okay. I'll take her." But he didn't. Hiding the hurt, she followed Stan to the elevator and stepped inside.

Daphne breathed in, breathed out.

Before they reached the main level, the elevator jerked and stopped.

"What's going on?" Daphne asked, as her brain fogged up with fear.

The lights blinked off. They were enveloped in darkness.

"You gotta be kiddin' me," Stan said.

"What's happening?" She couldn't think. Her hands flapped beside her like the wings of a jarred moth.

"It's okay, Daphne," he said in a soothing voice. "We're going to be fine. I'm trying to find the emergency switch. Someone will get us outta here soon."

Tears ran down her face and her stomach dropped out from under her. She felt like she might be sick. Then it occurred to her that this might be the exercise Cam had agreed to set up for Hortense Gray.

"This better not be an exercise. This isn't one of their exercises, is it?" She felt along the wall of the elevator for the rail, and when she found it, she held on tight.

"What are you talking about?"

"You know, therapeutic games? Cam knows I'm scared of elevators. It doesn't take a rocket scientist to figure out what's going on here. They're making me face my fear. Well forget this! Do you hear me out there? I don't like this one bit!" She hit her fist against the elevator wall.

"Calm down, Daphne."

"I thought therapeutic games would be like relay races and rock climbing. Scaring the crap out of me is not why I came!"

"What the hell are you talking about?"

"I'm sorry, Stan. This isn't your fault. Oh, God, oh my crap, I can't breathe!" She felt helpless, out of control, at the mercy of this stupid elevator and the way it was closing in on her, stifling her oxygen, trapping her, not letting her out. "Let me out!"

"Come here." He pulled her into his arms with a tight grip, forcing her to hold still. "Relax. It's okay," he said softly.

The lights flickered and then came on. The elevator dropped a few more feet to the bottom floor.

"Ahhh!" Daphne cried, catching against the wall.

The doors opened, and Daphne leapt out, trembling and angry and amazingly relieved. She avoided the eyes of the others in the foyer as she tried to regain control of her breathing and rushed from the building.

Stan caught up to her and put a hand on her shoulder just outside the main building. "You okay?"

She caught her breath and then said, "No."

"Let's head back to the rooms." He slid a hand behind her back and nudged her down the sidewalk.

"So, are they scaring the hell out of you, too?" she asked, after her breathing had returned to normal. "Any games as crazy as that?"

"What do you mean? What games?"

"Isn't Dr. Gray putting you through therapeutic games?"

"I'm here studying the Chumash Indian ruins and archaeological sites for a paper I'm writing."

Daphne stopped on the sidewalk near the pool, where the underwater lights had turned on, making the water glow in the dusk falling around them. "I don't understand."

Stan put an arm around her waist and pulled her onward. "If you ask me, Cam's just teasing you."

"No. Dr. Gray said so, too."

"Therapeutic games? What does that even mean?"

Daphne shrugged. "I don't intend to stay and find out."

They reached her unit.

"You just got here and made my trip one hundred percent better. I hate to see you leave."

Daphne blushed. "That's sweet." Maybe she just needed to draw a line for Cam. "Thanks. Maybe if I talk to Cam and the doctor..."

"There you go."

She unlocked her door. "Well, good night."

"Good night."

Daphne turned on the television, still shaken from the elevator. She reminded herself that she wasn't afraid of death. It was the pain she feared, and Cam wouldn't put her in any *real* pain or danger. She changed into her night shirt and hung up her clothes. She was folding the sheet back on the bed when the doorbell rang.

She peeked through the window to see who was there, but the window didn't give her a full view.

"Who is it?" she asked. When there was no reply, she asked again. The doorbell rang.

"Cam?" She returned to the window and this time was met by a strange, ghostly face looking back at her. "Ahh!" Daphne jumped back.

A young woman with two long braids and skin white as a ghost and blood-red eyes looked in at her. Daphne didn't know what to think or what to do, muttering, "What in the hell is going on?" Once she recovered from the shock, since she didn't believe in ghosts, and since she was pissed and wasn't about to let on that they had gotten to her with the elevator, she waved.

She was about to say, "How do you do?" with amusement when the door to her unit opened, and the ghastly figure stood in the doorway.

Daphne froze. Hadn't she locked the door?

The girl was covered in white powder and had bizarre red eyes. Red stuff dripped from them and from her blue lips. She wore a short black dress, torn in places.

"Are you one of the living or the dead?" The ghost carried an enormous shotgun.

"What?"

Before Daphne could react, the ghost girl pointed the gun and pulled the trigger. A spray of fine white powder shot out. Daphne closed her eyes to keep the powder from getting into them as the ghost girl ran out.

Daphne rushed to the door and closed it, locked it, and leaned her back against it just in case.

The ghost girl put her face to the window and screamed, "You are one of the dead! You hear me, Daphne Janus? You are not living! You are one of the dead!"

Daphne pulled at the curtain to block out the hideous face, but soon there were other faces, equally gruesome, peering in at her. Together they said, "You are not living! You are one of the dead!" The curtain panels wouldn't close over the entire window. There was a three-inch gap between them through which Daphne could still see the white faces and the red eyes and blue lips dripping with blood—fake blood, she reminded herself.

"You are not living! You are one of the dead!"

Daphne ran into the bathroom and closed the door. She stood there, shaking. What in the world had just happened? She looked at herself in the mirror. Baby powder. She was covered in baby powder. She might have laughed if she weren't so upset. In the bathroom, she used her towel to wipe herself clean. Then she poked her head through the bathroom door. The faces at the window were gone.

She checked the lock on the door and dragged one of the striped chairs in front of it, just to be sure. Then she phoned Cam, ready to give him an earful, ready to demand he take her home on the first boat, but he didn't answer, so she called the courtesy desk to leave messages for him and for Hortense Gray.

She turned on the television for a while, too keyed up for sleep. She waited for Cam for over an hour, checking the window now and then for those horrible faces. She took out her journal and tried to write, but nothing came to her. She just doodled all over the back of one page, making circles, then caterpillars, then leaves. At ten o'clock, she called Cam's room, but there was still no answer.

At some point, with the TV on, as she allowed herself to think of her sister, Kara, and her brother, Joey, and then of sweet, sweet, Brock and all they might have had together, and as tears slid down the corners of her eyes, she fell asleep.

CHAPTER FOUR

A Change of Heart

Daphne woke up early and peered out the window. One of the girls she met at dinner was sunbathing by the pool, eyes closed. A few other people walked on the sidewalks going to and coming from the main building and the beach. Daphne was peeved that Cam hadn't returned her call. She was anxious to see the look on his face when she told him about what had happened last night. She called him, but once again, there was no answer.

She took her bag from the closet and started packing. When she had finished, she went to the window and scanned the pool and sidewalks. People walked past, and a few more were on loungers. A man swam laps in the pool.

Seeing no sign of the ghost girls, Daphne put on her bathing suit to swim laps, too. Swimming had always calmed her. Plus, she wanted one more look at the underwater aquarium before demanding to be taken off the island.

Swimming on top of all that beautiful marine life was magnificent. She felt as though she were in the ocean as she navigated over the coral and sea urchins and colorful anemone, easier to see clearly now with her goggles. As she made her turn to continue freestyle to the other side, the moray eel poked out of the wall of the cave and snatched the silver flash of a fish. Other fish darted away, in the same direction as she, a whole school, and she was swimming with them, one with them, a part of the universe.

She climbed out of the pool and slipped on her cover, a silky yellow one with buttons. A few people she recognized from dinner were walking toward the main building for breakfast. Daphne preferred to have toast or muffins in her own room (she would never enter that elevator again), but first she wanted to take another look at the beach.

As she climbed the steps up the canyon wall, the wind knocked against her, adding to her overall feeling of rejuvenation. From the summit, the view was as spectacular as she had remembered it, with the yellow poppies dancing in the breeze to her left, and the chalky bluff, an impenetrable fortress, to her right. Circling above the bluff was a pair of bald eagles. Before she took her eyes away, they soared down toward the valley and were gone. Below her were the empty white beach and the gentle, foamy waves and a handful of gulls calling to her. She was about to turn and head back to her room when a figure on the chalky bluff caught her attention. Someone was standing there, looking out over the sea, and before she could make out whether it was a man or a woman, the figure flung itself over the edge and into the raging water below.

Daphne drew in air and stood there at a loss. Was the person crazy? Did whoever it was *want* to die? She couldn't decide whether she should run down to the beach and wait to see if the person made it to the shore or run for help. Several agonizing seconds passed before she decided to go for the beach, in spite of Arturo Gomez's warning to avoid going places alone. On her way down the steep boardwalk, she saw the person resurface and climb back up the chalky bluff as though he or she were a starfish scaling along the side of a cave.

When she reached the beach, the figure jumped once more. Daphne took off her flip-flops and jogged along the beach to the bottom of the bluff and waited for the person to resurface. Twenty feet away, a dark curly head emerged.

"Stan!"

He turned in mid-climb, grasping the base of the bluff. He waved, lowered himself back into the water, and swam up until he hit the shallow sand bed, where he climbed to his feet. She waded out and met him.

"What are you doing? You could hit your head on a rock and die out here. You shouldn't be out here alone."

"As it turns out, I'm not. You're here."

"You're crazy."

"Come on. Give it a try."

"No way. You scared me to death." The thought of her bones crunching against the sharp rocks below sent a shiver down her neck.

He gave her a charming smile. "I was about to head back. Have you eaten?"

"Not yet." She put on her flip-flops. The sand was hot. "I'm going to eat in my room."

"You're the one who's crazy. They have the best breakfast buffet here." They climbed the steps of the boardwalk. "Looks like you went for a swim, too."

"Not a crazy, cliff diving swim, but yes. Laps in the glass-bottom pool."

"Yeah. Nothing like it in the whole world."

"It's amazing. I saw a moray eel grabbing its breakfast."

"You sound happier today. Are you still planning on leaving?"

"Maybe. I don't know." Seeing Stan and having a normal conversation with him made her question her decision to leave. She waited for him to comment, and when he didn't, she asked, "Are you going kayaking this afternoon?"

"I want to, but I need to get a couple of days' work in. I've got to get this paper done before the summer ends, and I can't write the paper if I don't study the archaeological sites and ruins more thoroughly."

"Too bad."

"I was going to put it off, but we're supposed to be getting bad weather tomorrow evening, so I better do it today. You should come with me sometime. They're amazing."

"Do they have tours?" She recalled a family trip to Mesa Verde in western Colorado when she was seven. Kara was five and still alive and Joey had not yet started listening to the voices.

"Not yet. Someday they will, but now it's all still primitive on that side of the island."

They made their descent down the wooden steps, the wind railing against them. Daphne asked, "So did you have any visitors last night?"

He bent his brows. "Visitors?"

"Ghosts."

"You were visited by ghosts last night? What a night you had."

"Not real ghosts. I don't believe in real ghosts."

"Thank God. For a moment you had me worried."

She quickly skipped down the remaining steps, and he followed behind her.

"So, what kind of ghosts were they then?" he asked.

"People in costume, I guess. They didn't come to your door last night?"

"Not that I'm aware of. I didn't hear anyone."

They passed the pool and reached his unit. "This is me. Want to come in while I change?"

"No, I'm going to eat in my room."

"Goodbye, then."

She left Stan's unit to return to her own.

While in the shower, she decided to stay and carry out her original plan. She might not have another chance like this for a very long time.

Have you ever considered the possibility that there might not be a heaven? The voice inside her head asked.

Yes. In fact, I have.

She found muffins and fruit and juice in the kitchenette and brewed a mug of coffee and was finishing up when Cam rang at the door. She opened it.

"I missed you last night," she said, keeping her distance, unsure whether she wanted him to know how hurt and angry she was.

"I had a late night with Dr. Gray. Sorry."

She stepped away from the door to let him in. "So, you didn't get my message?"

"No. You left a message?"

"Last night. I was thinking of leaving today, but I've changed my mind."

"Leaving? Are you serious? Why? Don't tell me the game with the ghosts scared you. It was supposed to be a fun kind of scary, you know?"

She moved to a striped chair and crossed her feet on the coffee table. "The elevator."

"The elevator?"

She studied his face but found only confusion as she told him what had happened.

"I underestimated Stan," he said. "What a jerk."

"What? Jerk? No, Stan helped me. I was scared to death."

"Sure, he helped you. He stopped the elevator himself to frighten you into his arms."

"Impossible. I would have noticed. Plus, the lights went out." She could feel the heat on her face. Did Cam really think Stan liked her in that way?

"They probably shut off when you shut down the elevator."

"It wasn't Stan. I thought it was you and Hortense Gray."

Cam's jaw dropped. "What? How? We were still at dinner. How could we have done it? And why?"

"It wasn't one of your exercises?"

He crossed his arms. "The exercise was the ghosts. I thought you would like it. The same thing was done to me on my first night, and I loved it."

"By then I was too upset from the elevator."

"You've got to believe me, Daph. I had nothing to do with the elevator. Maybe Stan didn't either. Maybe it just got stuck."

"Has that ever happened before?"

"I don't know. Not to me." He plopped in the other chair beside her.

"Why doesn't Stan know about the therapeutic games?" she asked.

"They have regular guests here, too. Mostly students and scientists and archaeologists."

"I called you at ten last night."

"Dr. Gray put me through an exercise that ran late. It was bizarre. I'm not supposed to talk about it. She'll probably give the same one to you. It was awesome."

"Cam," she punched his arm. "Tell me."

He pursed his lips and made a motion with his fingers of locking his mouth shut.

She rolled her eyes and asked, "Are you still going kayaking?"

"Of course. The caves are amazing."

The phone rang. Dr. Gray was on the line, asking her to come to the lobby to meet with the naval guards. They needed to take down her statement about the girl and the man in the valley.

Apprehensive, she recalled the last time she had to give a statement. She had been the only witness other than Joey. She had wanted to lie then. Maybe she should have lied.

She met with the guards in the lobby where they sat in overstuffed chairs, and she told them what she saw. Hortense, Cam, and Roger were with her, corroborating her statement. The younger of the two took notes and the older, shorter one asked the questions. When she said all she knew, she asked the officers if they thought the murderer was still at large on the island.

"Doubtful," the older one said. "Unlike serial killers, who leave clues and hang around to watch the investigation, this guy appears to be an opportunist who took advantage of a situation. He probably got off the island as soon as he could."

"But you don't know this for sure?" Daphne asked.

"No. We're searching every square inch, but you've got to understand we have little to go on, and killers look like everyone else."

Cam put his hand over hers when the officers left. "Don't worry. I'll take care of you."

Daphne had the same intuitive feeling she had felt at dinner—that everyone around her was acting. She continued to suspect that there was no murderer, and the naval guards were actors, too.

Hortense thanked Roger for coming, dismissing him, and turned to Daphne. "I have a short and easy exercise for you, which I can conduct here at this coffee table." She gave Daphne a stack of index cards. "I'd like you to read the information on each of the cards and then sort them into categories."

"How many categories?"

"That's entirely up to you. Take as much time as you need."

She looked across the table at Cam, who gave her an encouraging nod. On each card was written the name of a color, but the ink in which it was written did not match the name in color. Daphne needed to decide whether to sort the cards by the names of the colors or by the colors of ink. Should she put the index cards with the word "red" in one pile, or the index cards in which red ink was used in one pile? Daphne went with the former.

When she finished, Hortense gave her another stack of index cards. "Once more, please."

Daphne wondered how these exercises could be considered "therapeutic." Maybe the doctor was gathering information about Daphne so she could design better games for her.

This time each card had a description of a death. The first read, "A boy is accidentally run down by a drunken driver." Another read, "A bank robber kills an uncooperative bank employee during a robbery." Daphne put the deaths into categories: unavoidable accidental deaths ("A man is killed by lightning"), avoidable accidental deaths ("An unsupervised child drowns in a swimming pool"), intentional deaths without premeditation ("A store clerk is killed when he tries to disarm a robber"), and intentional deaths with premeditation ("An adulterous woman is killed by her husband").

Daphne was moving right along, systematically placing the index cards, rather pleased with her speed, though she did not know if speed was a concern of the experiment (she had been told to take her time), when she came upon this on the very last card: "A mentally ill boy strangles his sister to death." Daphne looked from the card to Dr. Gray. Who was this woman?

She narrowed her eyes at Cam, who couldn't see the writing on the card.

"Are you okay, Daphne?" the doctor asked. "Is something wrong?"

With trembling hands, Daphne placed the card in the "avoidable accidental deaths" pile. "Fine. Finished. Are we done?"

"Yes. Thank you. I'll see you at dinner tonight."

Daphne and Cam got up and left the main building, Daphne unable to hide her shaking hands. She squinted in the bright sun.

"You okay?" Cam asked. "You seem upset."

She stopped and turned to face him. "What did you tell her? I thought you were my friend."

He reached out to her, but she pulled away and continued walking in front of him. She'd go back to her room and finish packing her bags. She had to get away from this place.

"Daph, wait."

She kept walking. "I want to go home."

"Hold on." He caught up to her and took her arm. "Please. Listen to me."

She stopped and glared at him. "Well?"

"I'll take you home in the morning, if you still want to go. There's no boat 'til then."

"Oh, Geez! I saw hundreds at Scorpion Anchorage."

"The boats connected with the resort dock only at Prisoners Harbor."

"Just great."

He took her hand. "For now, try and relax. Let's go get a massage. That should help."

"What did you tell her?" Daphne demanded.

"I told her what happened to Kara."

"Why?" she asked, tears welling in her eyes. She could barely see.

"I don't know. I'm sorry. I had no idea it would come up."

Daphne turned toward her cabana. Maybe she would move her plans up to tonight.

"So, no massage?"

"No. I'm going back to my room."

"Daph, I'm sorry."

She closed the door in his face and plopped on the bed in a heap of tears. She hadn't allowed herself to really cry out loud like this in a long time. The tightness in her throat and the burning in her chest felt good.

"You mean you heard and did nothing?" her mother had said.

Daphne screamed and thrashed against the bed covers.

The doctors said schizophrenia can be brought on by a traumatic event. Joey got it from accidentally killing Grandpa Janus. Maybe Daphne would get it, too.

Grandpa should have left a note warning them he had turned off the electricity at the feed and convenience store he owned and operated. He was in the attic repairing the air conditioner when Daphne's mom dropped off Joey to work that summer where their dad once worked when he was a boy. Joey, fourteen, his first job, called out for Grandpa. Joey thought he was in the back freezer or the storeroom, or further out at the silo or even the shed. When the lights wouldn't turn on, Joey tried another switch; nothing. The refrigerators weren't on. Nothing was on. He found the power breakers and pulled the switches. One by one, he brought everything back to life. The refrigerators buzzed, the florescent lights shined, the Icee maker turned the ice. Joey could not have known the funny smell coming from the attic was burning human flesh.

Later, Cam called and begged her to go on the kayak excursion with him. She was exhausted, but she decided to bite the bullet and go. Although she was angry that he'd told Hortense Gray about Kara, there was nothing he could do to deserve what she was going to do to him tonight.

A group gathered in a clearing where four jeeps were parked in the glaring sun. Daphne and Cam climbed in the hot, cracked vinyl seat behind Roger and an older man, early thirties, they didn't know. They exchanged greetings. His name was Phillip from northern California.

Roger drove them back to Prisoners Harbor, and they met their cave guide at the kayak rental. Daphne had expected the guide to be more like a blond California surfer, but instead, he was a heavy Native American with long black hair pulled into a ponytail. His bathing trousers were too large and sagged like the baggy jeans of an urban kid, revealing the top of his crack. The t-shirt had holes and stains, and was too short, allowing the hairy and protruding belly full exposure.

"I'm Larry," he said, shaking their hands.

Hairy Larry, Daphne thought. Then she recognized him from Hortense's dinner table.

Two other guys showed up in another jeep—Vince and Dave. They had sat with Daphne with the younger crowd at dinner. They were college-age boys. Vince was thin, blond, and pale—same color as Cam. He didn't talk much, and when he did, Daphne could barely hear what he was saying. Dave was the opposite. He was short, Hispanic, with a thick head of curly hair, and a loud, rambunctious voice. He laughed a lot, and half the time, Daphne didn't understand his jokes.

Larry helped them each choose the right kayak and life vest according to height and weight. He also gave them each a water bottle and a whistle. As they carried their kayaks to the harbor, Larry told them a few basic instructions: stay with the group; stay close to the shoreline; paddle at a diagonal to, rather than against, the waves; blow the whistle if you get separated from the group; don't throw your waste in the water; don't feed the wildlife; don't touch the ancient art and petroglyphs on the cave walls; remain in the kayak at all times.

"It's not dangerous, right?" Daphne asked, feeling nervous now that they were about to begin.

"Sure, it is," Larry said with a smile. "That's what makes it fun."

CHAPTER FIVE

The Caves

At last Daphne and the rest of the group were in the water and paddling along the coastline toward the first cave. Prisoners Harbor was full of boats cruising in and out, but none docked at the pier. As they passed Pelican Bay, the squawking made it impossible for a while to hear anything else. The wind whipped Daphne's ponytail against her shoulders and brought the fresh salt air all around her. Something rushed away from her kayak, causing her to jump in her seat, and when she realized it was an otter, she squealed, pointing and trying to get Cam's attention. It had such a cute face and was so close. She could reach out and touch it but didn't dare. The otter looked at her as he swam away on his back.

When they finally passed the boisterous babble of the birds, she told Cam about the otter, nearly falling out of her kayak as she tried to demonstrate how close the otter had been to her. As she laughed, she was amazed by how easy it was to be happy here.

Larry shouted in a "tour-guide" voice, "Soon we'll come upon the first sea cave, known as Twin Rocks Cave, because the entrance is flanked by two nearly identical rocks. My people, the Chumash, believed the twin rocks were at one time gods, Tumaiya and Mukata, sons of Hu-tash, or Mother Earth. Legend has it the two gods disagreed about whether humans should live forever. Tumaiya wanted humans to share eternal life with the gods, but Mukata felt immortality should be for gods only. They had a long battle but were equally matched, and the battle went on and on for years until Hutash took matters into her own hands. She turned her sons into the two rocks and compromised between their wishes. She made it so that humans would die, but their ghosts could come to dwell in this cave, and a few times a year, she allows them to wander the island for one full day. You see the twin rocks?"

They were as tall as a three story-building, but columnar. Daphne could see why a group of people would believe they were gods. At the very top, they rounded like a human head. Despite the tall rocks, the entrance to the cave was the size of an armchair. This made Daphne's mouth go dry. She had not imagined she would be going inside so small an opening.

Larry said, "We'll save that cave for our journey back. It's best to go to the furthest one first, while the tide is low. Then we can ride the tide as it comes in. The paddling will be easier."

As they passed the two columnar twin rocks, they saw a group of sea lions sunning on a rocky cliff. They were golden in color with dog-like faces, little flaps for ears, and long whiskers, white in the sunshine. They stared at the kayakers as they passed.

"We'll also skip by this cave coming up, known as Falls Cave, and start with the one called Platts Cave."

Daphne was glad when they came to the cave and could stop paddling. Being on the water in the kayak was pleasant with the waves rocking her to and fro, but her arms needed a break.

The mouth to the cave made a huge arch, like a tunnel for a train. Light shone in to the first part of the cave, revealing shiny, shimmering walls reflecting light off the water. Larry pointed his flashlight to shelves all along the side walls and explained they were used for storage by the Chumash. On the ceiling were carved figures of dolphins, sea lions, whales, pelicans, gulls, and foxes.

Cam splashed Daphne with his paddle, laughing. "Having fun yet?"

"Well, I was till you splashed me." She splashed him back.

"Hey, echo!" Dave shouted, his voice emanating throughout the cave. He laughed. "Echo!"

This time a bat scurried past Daphne and out into the bright light.

"Way to go, Dave," Cam said with sarcasm.

"Oops!" Dave laughed at himself. "Sorry little bat!"

They turned from the cave at Platts Harbor and headed back in the direction they came, toward the east. Larry had been right about paddling with the tide. It was much easier and faster going east.

Daphne had been ignoring the urge to use the restroom since they started, but now she could no longer hold it. Full of embarrassment, she told Larry.

"We'll have to pull up onto the next bank. There aren't restrooms. Just find a private place and go."

She followed him to the next beach—rocky, unlike the sandy one by the resort. They stepped from the kayaks and pulled them ashore. The guys turned to the water and pissed.

There really was no good place for a girl to go. Everything here was rocky, without trees, and wide open. Daphne searched around, thinking she wouldn't be able to go after all. Finally she found a grotto on the underside of a cliff. As she climbed down, she caught a glimpse of someone dodging by.

"Hello?" she called out.

No one answered. Daphne hiked beneath the cliff edge and around to the other side, in the direction of the other person. As she rounded the corner, she heard the shuffle of running footsteps against gravel. She raced up the hill only to catch the back of a girl with long red hair running away from her. Then the girl disappeared behind another boulder.

That was odd. Maybe she was seeing things. She didn't believe in ghosts. Could it have been a mirage?

Daphne climbed back down beneath the cliff edge, her heart hammering in her chest. Her shorts were wet and hard to pull down. Plus, her hands were shaking. This island gave her the creeps. Why would a girl be running around by herself out here? She finished her business and made her way back to shore, and they waded out from the shallows and helped one another into their kayaks. She decided not to mention what she thought she saw. She'd say something later to Cam when they were alone.

The middle cave also had carvings along the ceiling, but even more spectacular was the waterfall spilling down from a hole in the center. The rushing water roared and created an echo effect in the cave, making it difficult to communicate inside. They each paddled around the falling water, allowing it to splash icily on a hand or a foot. Daphne held out her hand and shivered from the cold. Although water had gotten into the bottom of her kayak, it wasn't nearly as cold as the falling water in the middle of the dim, sparkly cave.

Larry led them from Falls Cave back to the first, Twin Rocks Cave.

The opening seemed even smaller than it had on the first pass.

Although the mouth was narrow, the cave itself curved high overhead. Carvings in the ceiling of dolphins and pelicans sparkled in the dim light. Larry took out his flashlight and shone it on the more visible carvings.

A shaft of light shone in from a crack above and bore down on a rocky ledge of figures toward the back of the cave. These weren't carved or painted, but sculpted objects made of bone and shiny shells. The shells of their eyes sparkled in the light.

"The Chumash believe those figures were made by our ancestors a long time ago to represent our forefathers," Larry explained. "They may look scary, but the Chumash see them as guardians of the dead, like the animals carved above us, and the twin gods at the mouth."

They hovered together in their kayaks with their backs to the mouth of the cave, staring at the strange figures on the back wall above them. The figure in the middle stared directly at Daphne, and she had the strange sensation of rising up toward it and of the walls closing in on her, the cave getting smaller by the minute. Then a flutter near her kayak caused her to jump and squeal.

"A school of stingrays," Larry said.

"Cool!" Cam said.

"They have stingers," Larry warned. "You can touch the very tops of them but watch out for their tails."

Dave burst out laughing, but Daphne had no idea why. Maybe he was delighted by the stingrays.

Phillip leaned over and used his fingertips to brush the top of one swimming by him. "Do they tend to frequent these caves?" Phillip asked.

"They usually come in with the tide," Larry said, turning. "Oh no."

The others turned toward the cave entrance. The tide had completely blocked it. They might have seen it coming if the shaft of light coming in from above hadn't kept the cave awash with light.

A wave of panic overtook Daphne. She couldn't speak, could barely breathe. The walls of the cave closed in on her, trapping her, taking away her control. She looked at Cam, tears pouring from her eyes, waiting for him to say something.

Instead, Cam turned to Larry and said, "How long?"

"Well, there's roughly six hours between high and low tide, but within two, three tops, we should have a big enough hole to get back out."

"Can we abandon the kayaks and swim for it?" Phillip asked.

"These rocks have sharp edges. The tide coming in can really throw you into them. I think it's too dangerous. We're better off waiting it out."

"Dang, Larry," Dave said. "I thought you knew what you were doing, *hombre*."

Cam asked, "What if we swim out towing the kayak behind us?"

"It'll be impossible to get the kayaks out of the cave. They can't be submerged easily. It's too risky, both for us and the boats."

Daphne could tell the blood had drained from her cheeks. She might be sick. "Hold my hand?" she said softly to Cam.

He maneuvered himself closer to her and took her outstretched hand. But even with the warmth of his hand in hers, she was going to scream and kick if she did not get out of the cave soon.

Then a thought occurred to Daphne. Was this a therapeutic game? Had she been led to this cave and trapped in here on purpose? An experienced guide would not have let a tide trap them in a cave. She narrowed her eyes at Cam.

"What?" he asked.

She shook her head.

"I can tell stories while we're waiting," Larry offered. "Stories of my people."

Larry then told them the same story Hortense Gray had told Daphne on the jeep ride into the resort, about Hutash sending Misink, the guardian of nature, to come down and control the population of people, turning some of the men into dolphins and taking some of the young women on his rainbow bridge to be his brides.

He said, "Here's another legend: Although humans were not given immortality as Tumaiya wished, one person was brought back from the dead by Hutash's orders, a young woman named Limuw, the same name they gave the island. Limuw means 'in the sea.' The young woman, Limuw, was very sad for many days, and one day, she ate a poisonous herb to kill herself so she could leave the sadness. But Hutash was not yet ready for Limuw to die, so she came to the leaders of the tribe in dreams and instructed them to take Limuw's body and shave off all the hair. They were then to wrap her body in cloth dipped in the oil of a native herb called Joitsa. Hutash gave the people words to use while they waited for the oil to soak into the body. After the words were repeated three times, Limuw opened her eyes, at first angry for what they had done. She had wanted to die. But after some time, she was grateful for another chance at life."

Then, without warning, the light from the top of the cave went dark. Pitch black surrounded them.

"Don't panic," Larry said. "Let me find my flashlight."

"This is ridiculous," Phillip said.

Cam squeezed Daphne's hand. "It's going to be okay."

"The sun must have moved behind a cloud," Larry said. "It will come back. Be patient. I'll find my light. Where did it go? I can't even see right in front of my face."

Someone—Dave, she soon realized, said, "It's kind of spooky." Then he added, "Bwahahaha!"

Daphne wanted to scream. She hyperventilated. She felt something slimy touch her leg. "Ah!"

Cam massaged her hand. "It's okay. Nothing bad is going to happen."

If she could speak, she would say it already had.

"I'm right here," Cam said. "Talk to me."

She could not catch her breath.

"Daphne, talk to me."

"I'm okay." It was just a game. She could endure this.

Cam said, "If you think about it, it's kind of cool being in a dark sea cave."

Someone, probably Phillip, snorted.

Cam added, "If nothing else, being frightened makes you appreciate life. Don't you agree?"

"No." She could hear the others whispering about her, but she didn't care. Let them laugh. She wanted out.

"If you didn't appreciate life, you wouldn't be afraid. You wouldn't care what happened to you," Cam reasoned.

"You could still fear pain." The slimy thing touched her again. "Eeeehhh!"

"But you aren't in pain, are you?"

"You're not helping."

Cam squeezed Daphne's hand and asked again, "Are you okay?"

Stupid, stupid question. She refused to answer it.

The light moved back through the crack in the ceiling, allowing the stifling darkness to dissipate. She searched her kayak near her legs and found a strand of seaweed. Sighing, she concentrated again on her breathing exercises.

"Ah, here it is," Larry said, turning on his light.

"How much longer?" Daphne asked.

"Miss, we haven't even been in here an hour. At least one more hour must pass before we can get the kayaks through."

"What if we sing?" Cam asked. Then, he broke out in song: "Ninety-nine bottles of beer on the wall, ninety-nine bottles of beer, take one down, pass it around, ninety-eight bottles of beer on the wall."

Soon all the guys were singing the song loudly and cheerfully—even Vince, who rarely seemed to speak. Daphne had to admit this helped. She gave Cam a smile of gratitude in the dim light of Larry's flashlight as he continued singing in his boisterous voice.

They took turns singing other songs. Cam started humming the *Imperial March* from *Star Wars*. And the others joined in.

Except for Daphne. She focused on her breathing and fixed her eyes on the mouth of the cave. After what seemed like an eternity, the tide moved down, and they were able to crouch into their kayaks and maneuver safely out.

In the sunshine and the fresh air, Daphne shouted hooray. She felt joyful to be out and free. When they passed the sea lions basking in the sun, she shouted hello to them. She shouted hello to the sun. She shouted hello to the sky and the kelp and everything she saw.

As if it weren't already obvious to the others in her group she shouted, "I'm so glad to be out of that cave!"

Back in her room, alone, in the warm and pleasant jet streams of the shower, Daphne knew it had all been a game. She had wanted to call Cam out on it but hadn't. Why hadn't she?

Because she already knew what he would say: He would deny it just as he had denied his knowledge of the elevator getting stuck. She couldn't trust him. He was part of the mysterious nature of this strange therapy of Dr. Gray's. This thought made her sad, and her eyes filled with tears. Cam was her only friend, and she couldn't trust him. Not for the first time, she wondered if she had it in her to continue. What other exercises did the game makers have in store for her?

Luckily, the stairs were dry Sunday night when Cam escorted Daphne up to the dining hall. Stan was not at dinner but was camped on the west end of the island by the Chumash ruins. Daphne found herself missing his company, feeling like he was the only person who was normal and trustworthy on the entire island.

After dinner, she told Cam she wasn't going on anymore outings and that she planned to stay in her room until they left in the morning. He continued to act like the incident in the cave had been nothing but an accident, but he didn't push her to leave the room. Instead, they watched a movie together—*The Amazing Spiderman*— (one of their favorites). Afterward, she asked him to stay the night.

"I don't want to be alone," she said. She didn't think she could go through with her plan if she were by herself.

They were sitting in the striped chairs with their feet on the coffee table. He said, "I usually don't just sleep when I stay the night with girls, Daphne Janus."

"Well, I'm not any ol' girl, Cameron Turner."

"Do you talk to Brock?"

Daphne closed her eyes and sighed. "You know I don't."

"So, it's safe to say it's been a while since you…" he whistled.

She glared at him. "Shut up! You think…"

His eyes widened. "What, never?"

"Would you stop?" She kicked him, but not hard.

"Maybe you need a friend with benefits. That's all I'm saying."

He was too cute to be mad at. "You lost that chance when you brought me to this creepy island under false pretenses."

"So there was a chance?"

She shook her head and smirked. "You're my best friend. I never want to screw that up." A lump rose to her throat as she considered the possibility of having sex before she died. Perhaps it was an experience no one should live without. She studied his golden blue eyes, his thin lips, the sweet curve of his neck. She wouldn't mind pressing herself against his solid chest and losing herself in his arms. It could truly be her last hurrah. Her only one of that kind.

No, that would only make what she was about to do to Cam that much crueler. "Seriously, please stop."

"I'm sorry. Really." He gave her a penitent smile. "I'll stay. And I'll be good."

"Why did you bring me here? It's not what I was expecting."

"I wish you would trust me, Daph." He reached for her hand. "I had the most amazing experience here last summer. Life-changing. Dr. Gray is the best. Just give it a chance."

She narrowed her eyes but didn't say anything.

"How about a game of chess?"

"Like the old days?" She brightened.

"Yeah. What do you say? I've got a board back in my room. I'll be right back."

"Promise?" She didn't want him to go. "Nothing weird's gonna happen?"

"I promise."

She was uneasy until he returned with the chess board.

When she was about to beat him for the second time, she said, "You better not be letting me win."

"How insulting. Quit rubbing it in." He gave her a hurt look.

"Just checking."

"I haven't played in like forever."

"Neither have I."

She felt awkward, after what he had said earlier, when they decided to call it quits and go to sleep. She left the TV on, needing the background noise. Although she was conscious of Cam lying in the bed beside her, it took less than sixty seconds for her thoughts to wander to Brock.

As soon as Cam's breathing became shallow and regular, she slipped from the covers and crept to the kitchenette. She took one of the knives and went to the bathroom, where she closed and locked the door and turned on the light.

It was no kind of life having to face the ones you hurt day in and day out. She couldn't stand to look her parents in the eye and see their pain reflecting back at her. They blamed her. Her mother had even said so.

That terrible morning when Daphne had realized what had happened to Kara, she had screamed and fallen in a heap on the floor.

"It was Joey!" Daphne had said. "I heard him go in Kara's room. I heard banging."

Her mother's face had stretched into almost comical proportions, her eyes wide as she had asked, "You mean you heard and did nothing?" Daphne just now had this thought: Extreme responses to comedy and tragedy look the same.

Daphne had fallen in a heap on the floor and had wanted to curl up and die, too.

"You mean you heard and did nothing?" her mother had said. The words played over and over in Daphne's mind. "You mean you heard and did nothing?"

Kara would be alive if Daphne had gotten out of bed that night. And Joey probably wouldn't have gotten so sick. Everyone's lives were ruined because she had done nothing to save them.

But she'd been happy for the first time in two years here on the island. She thought the happiness came from knowing she would finally leave behind her miserable life and spare herself the pain of looking into her parents' eyes, and yet, now she wondered if there had been something more to it than that.

She saw her mother's wide mouth and her wide eyes, looking at Daphne with utter disbelief. "You mean you heard and did nothing?"

Her mother blamed her for Kara's death, even if she tried to pretend otherwise later. Kara was gone because Daphne had been too lazy to get out of bed. A silent scream pressed against the walls of Daphne's skull. She was the scream, and she wanted out.

She took the steel blade of the knife and held it to her wrist. From her internet research, she knew the jugular would be quicker, but she'd have to look in the mirror to get it right, and she was afraid to see her own face looking back at her. This way, she could lie on the floor and not have to fall and hurt herself. The pain would be brief, according to the research.

Soon she'd go into shock and feel nothing.

CHAPTER SIX

The Amphitheater

As Daphne held the knife to her skin, she heard a commotion in her room, and then Cam was at the bathroom door, knocking.

"Daph? I need to pee! Let me in!"

Really?

As she stood up and hid the knife in a drawer, she became aware of how fast her heart was beating and of how badly her hands were trembling, which was weird, because she had thought she was so calm.

"I'm going to piss on myself if you don't open this door!"

"Okay, okay!" She opened it and flew by him, heading straight for the bed. She didn't want him to see the state she was in, especially with the bedside lamp flooding the room with light.

That's when she noticed the front door was open.

"Cam?"

"Yeah?" he said through the bathroom door, which he'd left ajar.

She stepped backwards toward him, keeping her eyes on the open front door. "Why is the door open?"

She heard the toilet flush.

"Huh?" He stepped into the room. "Oh, I thought I was going to have to take a whiz outside." He closed the front door and locked it. "Sorry. Desperate times, and all that, you know…"

She narrowed her eyes again.

"Look at you!" he said. "You look like a ghost!"

"You keep saying that." She climbed into bed, avoiding his eyes, and turned off the lamp.

He crawled in next to her. "Come here, Daph. I promise I won't do anything but hold you."

His body heat both calmed and excited her as she laid her head on his chest and curled her body up against his. One of his arms was beneath her neck, his hand caressing her arm. He reached over and cupped his other hand to the back of her head in a way that was so comforting that tears formed in her eyes. She closed them and sighed, having been on the verge of hyperventilating, but his hands moving through her hair helped her to slow down her breathing and get a grip.

"Cam I…" she didn't know what she wanted to say.

He stroked her hair and whispered, "SShh, it's okay."

She felt herself melting, her muscles relaxing, the beat of his heart syncing with the beat of hers.

"I'm glad you came to this island with me," he said softly. "It's supposed to be fun. I'm sorry it hasn't been."

But she was having fun *some* of the time—more fun than she'd had in years. "I'm glad I came, too."

"Really?"

"Yeah. It's a beautiful place, and fun, too."

"But?"

She shrugged.

"Daph, don't you know what a beautiful girl you are? What a sweet, smart person you are?"

Why was he telling her this? Did he have some clue as to what she had tried to do just before he came to the bathroom door? If so, how? Was she giving off some kind of vibe?

"Don't you know how much your parents and Joey love you, and how much I care about you?"

She stiffened, not sure what to say, but mortified by the thought that he somehow knew. Why else would he say these things? "Quit getting all mushy. If you're trying to seduce me, it's not working."

He laughed and pulled her close against him. "Oh, Daph."

She kept her head on his chest, catching with one hand the tears that poured from her eyes.

They were quiet for a while, and then Cam said, "No matter how much you cook a Wookie steak, it always comes out Chewy."

She slapped his chest. "That's terrible!"

"Made you laugh."

And it had.

Daphne felt something poking her. She brushed it away.

"Daphne, wake up."

"Huh?" She opened her eyes to see Cam dressed and leaning over her.

"There's no boat out today," he said. "I'm sorry. I thought they came and went every morning, but apparently, they only come twice a week."

She stretched and stifled a yawn. "So, when's the next one due?"

"Tomorrow."

She looked at the clock by the bed. It was almost noon. "I gotta pee." She got up and went to the bathroom.

After she finished using the toilet, she washed her hands and looked at herself in the mirror.

She dried her hands and opened the drawer, where she had hidden the knife. It wasn't there. She reached her hand into the drawer and felt all around.

The knife was gone. The heat left her bones. Maybe Cam *had* known.

"I'm hungry," she said, as she crossed the room to the kitchenette.

"I can take you for lunch."

She opened the silverware drawer to find all of the knives had been removed. "Cam?"

"Yeah?"

"Did you do something with the kitchen knives?"

"What? Uh-uh. Why?"

She didn't answer.

"So, you wanna grab a bite?"

She didn't feel like putting on a happy face in front of other people. "I'll just fix a sandwich here."

He came up behind her and turned her to face him. He had a strange look in his eyes, like he was afraid.

"What's wrong?" she asked.

He gave her a hug and muttered, "Nothing." But before he released her, he stuffed a folded piece of paper into her hand and whispered, "Shh. We're being watched."

"What?" Her mouth dropped open.

"Shh. Don't react." He pulled away. Then he said in a normal volume, "I'll call you later. You okay hanging out here till dinner?"

"Where are you going?"

"I'm wanted by Dr. Gray."

"You sure you're okay?" Daphne didn't like the look on his face.

"I gotta go. I'll come by around five to take you to the show."

"What show?"

"There's a show at the amphitheater this evening."

"You don't seem happy about going."

He took her in his arms once more and whispered, "They're listening. I can't talk now." He pulled away, gave her a desperate look, and then ran off toward the main building.

She wanted to call out to him but was afraid. What in the world was going on? She closed and locked her door, her hearting beating fast. When she opened the paper he'd slipped in her hand, the first lines read: *Take this with you into the bathroom. It's the only place in the room they don't have surveillance.*

She looked around before hastening to the bathroom and closing the door. They've been watching her? This whole time?

She quickly read the rest of the note: *There's something you need to know. My mom sent me here last summer to try and help me through a difficult time. It worked. I loved it. I'm a volunteer this summer. Your parents sent you here because my mom told them about my experience.*

I need you to know that Dr. Gray wants to turn you against me as part of your therapy, so you'll be less dependent on me. They think I'm falling in love with you, and maybe I am, and maybe I've sort of always loved you, and that's not good for the program. I'm sorry I lied to you. I hope this place helps you like it did me. But things get bad before they get better. Love, Cam.

Daphne read the letter again, overwhelmed with conflicting emotions. Maybe he loved her? Her parents had sent her here? Cam may have meant to clue her in, but his letter further confused her about everything. *But things get bad before they get better.* This was a warning.

She couldn't hide out in the bathroom all day, so she eventually tore up the note and flushed it before returning to the striped chair to sip on a soda, self-conscious about her every action. The fact that she was being watched made it impossible for her to relax. Her eyes fell on Hercules slaying the hydra.

So her mother and father *had* sent her here, she thought again.

She had wanted to die last New Year's Eve night when she had swallowed all the Prozac (and the Tylenol just to be sure). Brock had given up on her, had said that maybe they needed a break. She hadn't blamed him, really. She couldn't stand to look at him because she was so ashamed. So ghastly ashamed. How could she live a happy life with Brock when her sister was dead, and her brother plagued by voices? It wasn't fair and it was all her fault. And Brock deserved someone who was allowed to be happy.

When Kara died, her mother had said to Daphne, "You mean you heard and did nothing?" She immediately apologized to Daphne, but the damage had already been done.

Mothers can be so cruel. Daphne wondered whether her mother had sent her to this resort for therapy or punishment. It had to have been her mother's idea. Her father would never have sent her here. But since Kara's death, her father had pretty much been a robot, doing whatever her mother said.

If her mother and father were behind this, then maybe she could endure whatever lay ahead. Maybe this was a chance for her to atone for her sins. Then she could die absolved.

By the time Cam called, Daphne had changed into a light summer dress and sandals, another new outfit from her mother. She still didn't feel like being around others, especially with this new revelation, but she would force herself to carry on. It was time to pay the piper.

As soon as she saw Cam's face, she knew she was not to refer to the note, so obvious was the warning in his eyes. She kissed him on the cheek to reassure him. She would not allow whoever was watching them to suspect Cam of breaking any rules. Then she recalled what he'd written about loving her, and she felt her face get hot.

"You look beautiful, as always," he said solemnly.

"You, too." And he was beautiful, she realized again. One of the most beautiful people she knew. And she was grateful that he was trying to help her, even though this bizarre place creeped her out. She knew he cared for her, and she felt warm and comforted by that knowledge.

Together they walked past the pool and tennis courts in the opposite direction of the beach, past the long string of cabanas and the clearing where the jeeps were parked. They ascended a narrow flight of concrete steps tunneling through rock, too tight for Daphne's comfort. In a moment they emerged onto a canyon ridge. Below them stretched twenty rows of stadium-style seats carved in the rocky slope of the canyon. Further down was a platform with the other side of the canyon wall as its backdrop. The entire amphitheater looked about fifty yards in diameter, half the size of a football field.

Daphne recognized the twenty or so people already seated in the audience. Hortense Gray sat with Arturo Gomez, Lee Reynolds, Mary Ellen, and Phillip closer to the top of the stadium, but Cam and Daphne didn't stop to say hello. In the middle were others she recognized, including Roger and some of the waiters from the banquet hall. She was surprised none of the younger crowd was there. Cam led her to the center front, where the stage was eye level.

"You sure you want to sit this close?" Daphne asked.

"It's not a splash zone or anything. This isn't Sea World."

Daphne could tell Cam was still upset, and this made her more frightened of what lay ahead. As they sat on the warm concrete seat with the hot sun beaming down on them, Daphne began to sweat from more than the heat.

Shortly, three people appeared at the right of the stage to the soft, slow chords of string instruments or a recording off-stage. The actors wore hooded white cloaks, concealing their identities. Their feet were bare, and Daphne immediately thought of a cult. As the music escalated, the performers made their way to the center of the stage, their backs to the audience. In the center back of the stage, an altar rose from the platform, probably by some hidden mechanical means. When the altar reached its full height, the music abruptly stopped with one swift boom of a base drum. The three performers turned to face the audience.

The middle actor sang a song of love and loss, to the sound of a piano. Again, Daphne couldn't tell if it was a recording or a live performance, but she recognized the voice. It was Larry from the caves, and she was surprised by the lovely sound emanating from the burly, crack-showing Chumash Indian. His smooth, low voice, in its melancholy words, made perfect pitch.

He sang:

I cannot stand to see

How I've hurt those close to me;

Ribbons of despair run from their eyes, their eyes.

And ribbons of despair run from my eyes, my eyes.
Don't look at me
Those of you once close to me;
The fire inside you slowly dies, and dies.
And the fire inside me slowly dies, and dies.

Daphne could have written those words, for they described precisely how she felt. In fact, they reminded her of one of her poems. She closed her eyes to stay off any more tears.

After Larry finished his song, and after the brief applause from the audience, he said, "Bring Limuw forward."

Two more figures, also in white and hooded, carried a stretcher from the opposite side of the stage, and Daphne wondered by their shape and size if they might be Dave and Vince. On the stretcher lay a girl about Daphne's age. Her eyes were closed, her arms crossed over her chest, as though she were dead. She wore the same white cloak as the others on stage. For a moment, Daphne had the strange feeling the girl was, in fact, dead.

One of the original three performers stepped forward and sang another song, but it was in another language, and, anyway, Daphne could no longer hear the words. She stared at the girl, anxious to see some sign that she was alive.

The cloaked figures laid the stretcher out on the altar.

The base drum beat steadily to the human voices as they joined the other singer.

Then Larry, with his face still concealed by the hood, stepped forward and said, "This is Limuw. She has taken her life, and our prayers are to Hutash. Hutash agrees it is not yet Limuw's time. She has given us a ritual to bring Limuw back to life."

Daphne was shocked to see the five performers each pull a pair of scissors from their robes and cut the bright red hair of the girl on the altar. They cut it down to her scalp and then used electric razors to shave her head, arms, and legs. Surely the girl on the altar was an actress and a willing part of the performance and not the girl Daphne had seen running near the grotto.

As the string instruments played a slow and haunting melody, the five cloaked performers rubbed oil and laid long strips of white cloth on her body and sang a second song in Chumash. Toward the end of the song, the girl opened her eyes. She sat up, stared in horror at the audience, rubbed her bald head, and shrieked.

"My hair! What have you done?"

The five actors knelt in front of her as she stood from the altar.

Then Larry said, "Limuw has risen from the dead. You were dead and now you are alive again."

A new melody rang through the amphitheater, this time uplifting, but the woman playing Limuw continued to look confused. Thinking she was either an excellent actress or a victim of a strange ritual, Daphne shivered in the blazing sun and began to feel faint. When the melody ended, the five figures each put a hand on Limuw, and the members of the audience applauded. Many of them gave a standing ovation, and nearly all had tears in their eyes. Before the applause came to an end, the five performers escorted Limuw backstage behind a building of stacked stones, where the orchestra or the sound system must have been.

"That was different," Daphne said.

Cam stood and took her hand. "Let's go to dinner." As they walked up the stadium-style seats he added, "This might be hard for you to believe: Everybody in the audience this evening but you has played the role of Limuw."

"You're kidding! Even you?"

"Last summer. It was awesome."

"Well, I'm not doing it."

"No one wants to, but everyone's always glad they did."

"Not me." She couldn't imagine why any of them would be glad about having their head shaved.

Then a chill made goose bumps appear on her arms as she recalled the bald woman on the pier at Prisoners Harbor. Maybe it hadn't been chemotherapy. Maybe she'd been Limuw. And maybe the way she had grabbed Daphne's wrist and had given Daphne that strange look had been an attempt to warn her.

Daphne crossed her arms in front of her chest as Cam led her away from the amphitheater.

They reached the canyon ridge and followed the narrow steps back down to the main part of the resort. As they passed the jeeps, Cam said, "Some of the others are doing another exercise with Limuw right now. It's the best part. I'm supposed to be there, too, but I didn't want to leave you alone."

"Why can't I go with you?"

"First you have to be Limuw."

"That's not happening. Cam, seriously. How could getting your body hair shaved off be a rewarding experience?"

"You'll see."

"Not in this lifetime."

When Cam said nothing more, she asked, "They won't force me, will they?"

"I don't think so. They don't do it until the end of—" he stopped, looking past her. "We'll talk later."

Daphne looked around but saw no one close enough to overhear them. Then she realized, as they walked through the grounds, that there could be surveillance cameras hidden in the nearby buildings.

After an uneventful dinner, Cam asked her to walk down to the beach with him.

Far off to their right, the sun was setting, and at the top of the wooden steps, Daphne stopped to take in the beauty. Whatever else the resort was for the people who came here, it was first and foremost a beautiful place that brought much pleasure. Daphne suspected this was an important part of the resort's therapeutic qualities. She and Cam followed the boardwalk down to the sand, where they abandoned their shoes and strolled to the edge of the water. One other couple sat together in the sand by the hill of poppies and a lone woman stood at the top of the chalky bluffs gazing out to sea.

"They can still see us down here, but they can't hear what we're saying." Cam faced the sea.

The sun nearly touched the horizon and sank further by the minute. Orange hues reflected on the graceful waves. The wind was less violent down here near the water than it had been on the boardwalk.

"So my mother put me up to this? She set me up? And my dad?"

Cam nodded. "They've been worried about you."

Daphne hadn't looked her parents in the eye in months. It had been just like the words in Larry's song. "How did you find out about this place?"

"My mom knows someone who knows someone who knows Dr. Gray. I'm sorry I lied to you. I was told it was necessary to your therapy."

"I don't see how lying can ever be a good thing."

Cam said nothing.

As they continued down the beach toward the sunset and the chalky bluffs, Daphne asked, "So what was your rough time? Did you try to, you know..."

"No, but I came close. I guess I wasn't as brave as you."

Daphne sucked in her lips. It hadn't been bravery.

"I wasn't dealt as tough a hand as you," he said. "I never told you this, but I got into drugs and failed my first semester of college. My step-dad cut me off, even though the money comes from my mom. She supported his decision. I had nothing—no one, no friends, no job, no life."

"What about me?"

"Kara had just died the year before. I didn't want to bring you down again."

"Cam…"

"Anyway, it was a hard time. I finally agreed to go to rehab. This place was part of it. It made me realize how much I wanted to live, and how great life can be if you let it."

"I knew it. Getting trapped in the elevator and the cave, those things were therapeutic exercises, weren't they?"

He nodded. Then he faced her. "You have to admit they were exhilarating, like a roller-coaster ride."

It had all been creepy, but now that she knew for sure that she'd never been in any real danger, she was filled with relief. "I'm not much into roller-coasters." She gave him a smile. "But if this place helped you, then it can't be all bad."

"Then you're not angry at me?"

She shook her head.

"The whole bit in the valley with the woman being raped and killed was part of it too."

Daphne knew it. It had been a cruel trick, but she was glad it hadn't been real.

His smile quickly became a frown. "After tonight, Dr. Gray doesn't want me to interfere with your progress. She's putting distance between us."

"I don't like that." She grabbed his hand and filled with anxiety. "What are they going to do to me?"

"Trust me, Daph. Do you trust me?"

She nodded.

"It's going to be okay. You'll see."

Then she asked, "Was Stan in on the elevator incident?"

"No. He doesn't know it yet, but someone has sent him here, too."

"Who?"

"I don't know."

So Stan was a patient like her. "I suppose it has been fun," she said, which wasn't a lie. This was a major gesture on her parents' part. A lump formed in her throat. "But I'm scared."

"And excited?"

"I guess so. Yes." She had to admit she'd felt more alive the past two days than she had the past two years.

"It gets better."

"I won't be Limuw, though. I'd like to keep my hair."

"Okay, but it does grow back. It's just hair."

"What's the point?"

"It's not why, but what."

"Huh? What's that supposed to mean?"

"It has to do with living life to the fullest. It's about *what* life has to offer, and not *why* it does or does not offer certain things."

"And you have to be bald to do that?"

"It's symbolic. It gives you the chance to start over."

"I don't need to be bald to do that."

"Starting over isn't easy. Letting go is hard."

"Yeah." She leaned over and picked up a sand dollar, perfect except for one chipped edge.

"Sometimes it's hard to forgive yourself. Sometimes it takes something really dramatic and painful to help you let go of your mistakes."

She threw the sand dollar as far out to sea as she was able. "I guess."

"This place has another name." Cam stopped and put his hands on her shoulders, his eyes intently looking into hers.

"What?"

"The Purgatorium. Don't let on you know."

Daphne didn't know what to say, but sometimes when you're burdened with deep thoughts, the only thing left to do is to be ridiculous, so, after a moment, she said, "Let's go for a swim."

"Now? Here?"

"Why not?"

"In our clothes?"

"Strip down to your underwear. I don't care who's watching. Come on!" She pulled off her dress and ran out until the water reached her waist, then she dived in and swam a few strokes, feeling refreshed and revived.

Cam was close behind her. She turned to him and threw herself on him, dunking him under. They laughed and played together like they had the day she arrived.

That night, Cam didn't stay long, so she showered and put on her night shirt and lay in bed, thinking of everything she'd been told. She still couldn't believe her parents had sent her here. Maybe they really did want her to live.

Her thoughts eventually drifted to Cam, how much she liked him. He'd been her best friend forever, and now he admitted that he might be in love with her. Could she ever feel the same way about him?

As soon as she considered the possibility, her heart longed for Brock.

The first time she and Brock kissed was the week after his mother died. His mother had fought a five-year long battle with breast cancer and lost. Brock was an only child and was close to his mother. His father had left before the cancer, had moved to Philadelphia and had started another life that didn't include Brock.

Daphne saw the hurt in Brock's eyes when he came up to her in the parking lot after swim practice in early March her junior year. She didn't know what to say, so she stood there, listening.

"You should have seen her," Brock said. "She looked good."

"She was a beautiful woman. I'm sorry I didn't go to the funeral."

"It's okay. I was in a daze anyway."

"How are you now?"

"Still in a daze." He sort of laughed.

"Wanna grab a bite to eat together?" Daphne couldn't believe she had asked him on a date. The invitation sort of blurted out of her mouth without her realizing it.

"Sure."

Later, when he walked her to her door, she took him in her arms for a hug and felt him shudder, felt him lose himself. He cried, the hurt little boy that he was, even as his trembling hands reached for her face. Daphne was helping him to let go of the past by starting something new. She did it for him without realizing she would eventually have to hurt him.

CHAPTER SEVEN

The Sunset Cruise

The next morning, Daphne returned to the glass-bottom pool to swim laps. At one time, she swam a mile daily. Today she settled on half, choosing to dive down to admire her company. As she swam, she thought more about Cam, and the sweet way he had held her the night she nearly offed herself. Then she thought about Brock and the pain in his eyes when he finally gave up and said they needed a break.

Three schools of fish swam in different directions over the colorful coral, sponges, and sea anemone lining the reef. The yellow and white striped fish were the largest in number, but the electric blue were bigger and took up about as much room. Above them floated four tiny creatures Daphne believed to be jellyfish. There was no sign of the moray eel, but another creature slithered along the very bottom of the reef, rust-colored, and odd looking. Before Daphne could get a better look, a silky flash of silver darted into view and took the odd creature in its mouth. The silver flash came from a small shark. It circled the perimeter of the reef cave and then left as quickly as it had come.

After a shower and a bite of breakfast alone in her room, Daphne tried to reach Cam, and even knocked on the door to his room, but he didn't answer. Next, she tried Stan's room, but found no answer there either. So, having nothing better to do, and knowing there wasn't a murderer roaming the island dragging unsuspecting victims by the hair, she took a walk on the beach to enjoy the rising sun. It was a golden circle of warmth above the hillside, which was itself golden, covered in yellow poppies. Two people sat together at its apex on a blanket picnicking.

She neared the end of the beach, where pristine sand gave way to the steep, grassy hillside, and as she turned to walk back, a peal of laughter made her glance over her shoulder at the couple. She shielded her eyes from the sun. The guy was attempting a handstand. As she looked more carefully at the golden skin of the boy, his blond highlights made brighter by the sun, she realized it was Cam, picnicking with another girl. This must be Hortense's doing, her way to keep Daphne and Cam apart. But how could anyone have known Daphne would be walking the beach this morning? Daphne hadn't known herself until moments before she came. She thought it best to ignore them, regardless of their reasons for being there, and headed back to her room.

So much for being in love with Daphne. Despite herself, she was hurt. She'd grown fond of the idea that maybe Cam had deeper feelings for her.

She found *Gone with the Wind* and took it poolside to bathe in the sun. One other girl about Daphne's age lay on the opposite side, in a red bikini, apparently sleeping, her skin nearly as red as her suit. Daphne thought she recognized her from dinner and considered waking her, in case she hadn't meant to burn, but decided to mind her own business and began to read.

Before Daphne had gotten very far, the girl in the red bikini sat up, twisted her long brown hair up into a clip, took her towel from the back of the chair, and slipped her feet into her flip-flops. She stopped near Daphne and said, in a low voice, "They're using you, you know."

"Excuse me?"

The sunburnt girl looked around as though worried she was being watched. Then she leaned in close to Daphne's ear and said, "Did they tell you they were helping you? Told me the same. I've been here a month now. I ask all the time for a boat off the island. They keep putting me off. We're stuck here until they tire of us."

"I think I'm here for therapy," Daphne whispered.

"They'll tell you anything to keep you here. It's not a bad life, as long as you don't take it too seriously, and as long as you have nothing going for you on the mainland."

She didn't believe her, but she wanted to ask her some questions. "I'm Daphne."

"I know. We met. Emma." Then the girl looked up, startled.

Daphne turned in the direction of Emma's gaze to see Hortense Gray walking toward them. She wore a pair of khaki pants, a white long-sleeved shirt with a colorful scarf around her neck, and a forced smile.

"I've got to go," Emma said. "Good luck."

The doctor and Emma exchanged greetings as Emma passed. Then Dr. Gray came and sat down on the white lounger next to Daphne's feet.

"How are you today, Daphne?"

"Confused."

"I should have warned you when you first arrived. I have real patients here on campus undergoing therapy. The woman you spoke with just now is one of them. Unfortunately, she suffers from delusions. You have to take whatever she says with a grain of salt."

Daphne wasn't sure if she could believe the doctor. Was this another ruse?

"Cam is also a patient, though he's progressed wonderfully since last summer," Dr. Gray added.

"He told me."

"Oh? That surprises me."

"Why?"

"Because he's been in denial for so long. I'm glad to hear he recognizes he still needs help."

"But I thought…" Daphne stopped, worried she might accidentally betray Cam's confidence. "Never mind."

"I'm glad I ran into you, because I've wanted to ask if you've been enjoying your stay and the exercises we've put you through."

"For the most part, yeah."

"Good. I'm so glad to hear it. A group of guests about your age is taking a sunset cruise this evening after dinner. Perhaps you'd care to join them."

"Sounds nice."

"Meet up at the jeeps around seven-thirty and you'll be taken out to dock from Willows Anchorage, our own private pier."

"Great. Thanks."

Hortense climbed to her feet and said goodbye, but before she walked away, she said, "Daphne, just remember it's not 'why' but 'what.'"

Daphne narrowed her eyes, as Cam had told her the exact same line.

"Just think about that."

Hortense then left Daphne alone by the pool.

Daphne truly was more bewildered than ever. Maybe Hortense meant to undermine Cam's credibility by insinuating he was still a patient in need of therapy. For now, Daphne held to this belief, keeping her faith in Cam.

All through dinner, Daphne looked for Cam and was disturbed to see no sign of him. She sat at the younger crowd's table with Emma, who talked about being jilted by a boy in London last year. Daphne half-listened, unsure whether anything she said could be believed. She did not, however, notice any signs Emma was delusional.

Daphne considered herself somewhat of an expert on delusional people, having lived so long with her brother, Joey, whose own delusions began when he was around fourteen years of age, after their grandfather's death. Who knows at precisely what point his childhood games and creative imagination became sick psychosis?

If only Daphne had gotten out of bed that night. If only she had gone to check on Kara.

"Excuse me, Emma," Daphne said when there was a pause in Emma's monologue. "I'm suddenly not feeling very well. I think I'll go back to my room."

"I'll walk with you."

Not wishing to be rude, Daphne smiled and said okay, and they left the dining hall and took the stairs down to the main floor. As they passed the lobby, Cam and the girl from the picnic entered an elevator together. The doors closed on them just as Cam noticed Daphne. Daphne waited a moment, thinking he'd open the doors and come out to say hello, but when he didn't, she and Emma went on. Daphne's stomach formed a knot, and she wanted to cry.

"I feel like I've been hogging the conversation," Emma said as they walked by the pool and tennis courts. "Tell me. Have *you* ever been in love?"

"Yes. Once."

"What was his name?"

"Brock."

"Nice name. How did you meet?"

They reached Daphne's door. "Do you want to come in for a bit?"

"Sure. If you don't mind."

They sat on the striped chairs.

"Do you want a soda or anything?" Daphne asked.

"No thanks. I'm full from dinner."

"Me too."

"So tell me about Brock. After all, I've gone on and on all evening about Drew."

"The first time I met Brock, a kid threw up on my foot."

"Yuck."

"We were both on the high school swim team. He was a senior and I was a junior and we had gone to mentor some elementary kids after school. I'd seen Brock around, but we never really talked. We were in the library at the elementary school sitting at tables reading with the kids, helping them with their homework and stuff for community service hours when this second grader leaned over and threw up all over my shoe."

"What did you do?"

"It's funny, because I sat there for a minute, like a statue."

"Poor thing."

"Before I could react, here comes Brock with a towel. He squats at my feet, removes my shoe, cleans my foot, and then takes my shoe to the bathroom to rinse it under the sink."

"That's sweet."

"No guy had ever taken such good care of me before."

They laughed.

"Was it love at first sight?"

"It was for me."

"So did you ask him out, or did he ask you out?"

"I guess I asked him, but not for months after that happened with the kid."

"Why'd you wait so long?"

Daphne didn't know how to explain what it was like to feel bad about being happy. "I don't know. But when his mother died, well, I felt bad for him."

"Are you two still together?"

"No."

"What happened?"

"It's a long story. I don't want to get into it."

"We should head out to the jeep. You are going on the cruise, right?"

"I guess so."

Daphne and Emma were the first to arrive at the clearing, even before Roger, but he wasn't long after them. He said good evening and climbed behind the wheel of the jeep, waiting for one other to arrive before heading out to Willows Anchorage. A second jeep full of people gathered behind them and left shortly after. Daphne recognized Vince and Dave with another boy she hadn't met but was disappointed not to see Cam among them.

They drove up the canyon ridge toward the valley, but doubled back, curving around the amphitheater, and headed south, west of the chalky bluffs. The air was muggy this evening, but there were no clouds in the sky, and the sun baked them. Sweat pooled around her hair line, and she wiped it with the back of her hand.

Willows Anchorage was a short dock, half the size of Scorpion Anchorage, and a quarter of the pier at Prisoners Harbor. Sparse blades of grass grew between the rocks along the trail. One boat, a catamaran, drifted in the harbor, and as the party neared the dock, the boat moved toward them. The first to board was the new boy. He had black kinky hair and black eyes, and his skin was the color of weak coffee. He held out his hand and helped each of them onto the boat, giving them a charming smile.

"Gregory Gray," he said to Daphne as he helped her board. "Nice to meet you."

"Daphne Janus. Are you…?"

"Yes. Hortense is my mother."

As the boat pulled from the dock, two more ran down the trail from the jeeps calling out to the boat.

"Wait for us!"

Cam held the hand of the girl from the picnic, as blond and tall as he, clinging to her sun hat, her slim legs visible through the thin cloth of her sundress. She had beautiful lips and a small mole on her right cheek.

"This is Bridget," he said when more introductions were made.

Daphne expected Cam to say something to her, something to indicate he was her best friend, and when he didn't, she assumed he couldn't because he was told to keep a strict distance from her. Although she couldn't blame him for following the doctor's orders, it bothered her that he was so friendly with Bridget, and she hated herself for it.

Daphne stood between Emma and Gregory, striking up a conversation with the latter.

"How come I haven't seen you before?" Daphne asked.

"I only arrived this evening. Have you been here long?"

"A few days. Do you work for the resort?

"No. Just visiting. And you? Are you a guest or an employee?"

"A guest." She wanted to say, "prisoner," but she held her tongue.

"I hope you enjoy your stay." His eyes were like chocolate pudding—deep and sweet. She instantly liked him and felt he was nothing like his mother.

The whole group seemed in a joyful mood of hyper-excitement, including Emma, who now took over the conversation with Gregory, turning on charm Daphne hadn't yet witnessed. Daphne couldn't resist taking the opportunity to steal surreptitious glances at Cam, who continued to give Bridget his full attention.

Why did she have to be so beautiful?

Now Cam was pointing to a distant rock. Daphne followed his finger to see a group of sea lions sunning there. Despite her foul mood, she was delighted by the animals and clapped her hands, asking if they could get a closer view. Cam turned to her, giving her a brief smile.

So his indifference *is* an act, she thought.

The sun was a large golden orb quickly descending to their right, casting colors across the sea. Although the air was still muggy, the moving boat generated a pleasant breeze that kept them all from suffocating.

The group was disappointed not to see whales, but the sea lions kept them well entertained, until suddenly Bridget was pulling her dress over her head and leaping from the boat in her underwear.

"Is she allowed to do that?" Daphne asked Gregory.

"I don't see why not."

Cam's full attention returned to Bridget, and he laughed with joy, slapping his hand against his thigh. "I can't believe she did it!" he said. "Look at her!"

The boat idled in place so as not to leave the swimmer behind. Before Daphne thought twice about it, she pulled her dress over her head and followed Bridget in.

I'm such a child, she thought, tugging her bra strap back to her shoulder, ashamed of herself, but she had to admit the water felt great, and, surprisingly, the sea lions hadn't left their rock. They looked at her with curiosity. She swam closer to them, leaving Bridget in her wake.

The others were shouting at her, but she couldn't tell what they were saying. She suspected they were cheering her on, and she was happy she had stolen the show, if even for a moment, from Bridget. She was determined to get closer to the sea lions.

When she looked back at the boat, she saw Bridget being helped back in, and the rest of the group shouting toward her. They were pointing, probably at the sea lions. Daphne gave them a thumbs up as the boat moved toward her. She looked again at the sea lions when something hit her on the head. It was a life buoy. She turned to the boat to see the entire group leaning over the rail screaming at her, pointing. At the sea lions?

Then Daphne saw the dorsal fins of the sharks about ten feet away. There were three of them. Her mouth fell open, and she stopped kicking. She imagined the jaws chomping her body in half, or worse, taking her limbs one by one with her mind still conscious. What a way to go. So many times she had fantasized about her death, but being pulled apart by sharks hadn't crossed her mind. Now, faced with that possibility, she felt the air leave her body, a vice grip her throat, and the scream, lodged there, stifled. She was going to die. But first, she was going to have to endure extreme torture.

She held on to the buoy and realized Cam and Gregory were pulling her in with all their strength as the captain sped away from the sharks with the boat. She was spinning through the water, in a blind and panicky delirium, unable to see or hear or think.

It wasn't until she was safely on the deck of the pier, down on her knees sucking in air and trembling, that it occurred to her the sharks might not have been real. They could have been divers with fins strapped to their backs, actors in yet another terrifying game.

She was given a towel and a great deal of sympathy and helped by Gregory and Cam from the pier to the jeep. The slight smile on Cam's face as he left her to join Bridget reinforced her suspicion that it had been a game, and Bridget had been one of the actors, in on it from the beginning. Daphne wondered how it all would have played out if she hadn't gone in the water. Perhaps someone would have pushed her in, unless the sharks were meant for Bridget. Daphne suspected she had reacted predictably to Cam and Bridget's behavior. Was she really so easy to manipulate?

CHAPTER EIGHT

Hortense Gray

After a sleepless night alone—Cam had answered none of her calls and had seemed to vanish from the island—Daphne received a phone call from the girl at the courtesy desk asking her to come in a half hour to Dr. Gray's office on the second floor of the main building, room 200. Daphne hadn't planned on going to breakfast—there were still plenty of fruit and things in her room—but now she quickly showered and dressed, wondering what this was all about. She supposed she could refuse to go, but she had to admit she was curious to know why the doctor wanted to see her.

She slipped on another one of the sundresses her mother bought her for the trip, put on her sandals, and headed over to the main building. The pool was full of swimmers and sunbathers, including Gregory Gray and others from yesterday's sunset cruise—all but Cam. She avoided making eye contact with any of them as she shuffled by, quickly, hoping they wouldn't notice. She wasn't in the mood to be around people.

She climbed the stairs to room 200. She lifted her hand to knock but hesitated when she heard opera music coming from the other side of the door. In a low vibrato, and in a language that sounded like Latin, Hortense Gray's voice rang out, and it was not good. Daphne covered her smile with her hand and listened until the music stopped, and then she raised her hand and rapped on the door.

"Enter."

Daphne gasped before she had even crossed the threshold, because the doctor's office wasn't anything like what she had expected. Every square inch of wall space was covered with either bookcases overflowing with books or with paintings from many different eras and styles, looking gaudy and crammed together. In the middle of the room were sculptures—three free-standing, life-sized ones and two smaller busts on pedestals. A loom sat in one corner with threads and a half-woven tapestry, and stuffed in another corner was an upright piano, covered in sheet music, some of which had fallen to the floor.

The doctor stood behind her desk wearing a large purple hat and purple velvet suit, which looked ridiculous. She lifted the needle from an old-fashioned record player, plunked on one corner of her messy desk, and removed a record and slipped it into a paper sleeve as she said, "Well, don't just stand there. Come in and have a seat."

Daphne had to weave around the many pieces of art to reach the green chenille chair in front to Dr. Gray's desk, and before she could sit on it, she had to remove a painting.

"Oh, just put that over there on the piano bench. I haven't decided where I'm going to hang that one. Do you like it? It's a Pre-Raphaelite imitation. A recent gift from a patient."

The painting was of a woman in a beautiful dress lying in a stream on her back with flowers all around her. She only had to lay her head back to be completely submerged.

"Is the woman going to drown herself?" Daphne asked as she carefully sat the painting on the piano bench.

"I guess we'll never know. That's the thing about paintings. They're frozen." After Daphne had taken her seat, the doctor asked, "Do you like my costume?"

Daphne was relieved that it was a costume. She hadn't been sure how to take the purple hat and suit and white bowtie. "Yes."

"I'm the mad hatter; can you tell? We're having a costume party in the ballroom next week, and I've been trying to decide how to dress. I think this one suits me."

"Yes," Daphne agreed. "It does."

Hortense Gray removed the purple hat from her head and tossed it on the floor behind her desk. "Well, now." She sat down and opened a manila folder on the top of a heap of folders. "Thank you for meeting with me. I wanted to discuss a few things with you. First of all, I wanted to tell you how sorry I am about what happened yesterday evening during the cruise. Gregory told me. You must have been terrified."

Dr. Gray wore a strange smile that made her words seem insincere.

Daphne shrugged and asked, "So why am I here?"

"Interesting question and one we all ask from time to time, don't you think? But as I like to say, 'It's not why but what,' for life's meaning isn't something assigned to us but rather made. Therefore, it's not why we are here, but what we do with our lives that matters."

What? "I mean, why did you ask me to your office?"

"Oh, yes, of course." She removed the bowtie from her neck. "You and I haven't had much time to chat. I want to make sure you understand a few things about my domain."

"Your domain?"

Hortense laughed. "That's my little inside joke. I like to think of myself as Prospero. Are you familiar with Shakespeare's *The Tempest*?"

Daphne shook her head.

"Well, it's very good. You should read it. In fact, I have it here somewhere." Hortense crossed the room to one of her bookcases, ran her finger along the spines of several books, and then stopped on one and pulled it into her hands. "You see, I've created a place where science, art, and even religion come together in one cause." She chuckled. "Nietzsche would be impressed. Here. Take it. You can keep it."

Daphne took the book from Hortense's outstretched hand. It was a black leather-bound copy and not too thick. She doubted she would have time to read it, but she didn't want to appear rude. "Thank you."

Hortense returned to her high-back leather chair behind her desk. "I want you to know there's very little that happens on this island that I'm not aware of. I know Cameron shared some information with you, and I wanted an opportunity to explain."

Daphne's heart rate increased, and she sat up in the chair. "He's not in trouble, is he?"

"Of course not. This isn't a school and he a pupil. Do you see me as a strict principal? How interesting. No, maybe you see this as a prison and I the warden? Cameron's a volunteer. This is a therapeutic retreat. Relax."

Daphne sat back in her chair.

"I want you to understand that I come from generations of psychologists. My father was a great psychologist, and his father before him, and so on. Have you heard of the Stanley Milgram Experiment?"

Daphne shook her head.

"What about Philip Zimbardo's Stanford Prison Experiment?"

"No. Sorry."

Hortense shook her head in disgust. "What do they teach kids in school these days? That's a shame. Well, my father, Malcolm Gray, was one of a great generation of psychologists back in the sixties and seventies who discovered important insights into human behavior. Stanley Milgram's shock experiment…"

"Wait, he shocked people?" Daphne asked.

"No. But he made the subjects *think* they were shocking people, and he discovered that the majority of his subjects would continue to obey authority even in the face of begging and pleading on the part of the actor pretending to be shocked."

"That's horrible."

"The behavior, yes, but the experiment was brilliant." Hortense leaned back in her chair and steepled her fingers "You see, this generation of scientists were trying to explain how regular German citizens could have participated in the annihilation of over six million Jews during the Second World War. You are familiar with the holocaust?"

"We learned about it in school." Plus, Daphne had read several novels on her own, such as *The Boy in the Striped Pajamas* and *The Book Thief* and *Number the Stars*. She shuddered. "It doesn't seem real."

"Yes, but it was real. And so psychologists wanted to study how such atrocities could be committed by everyday people. Zimbardo was another of my father's colleagues who created a remarkable experiment by simulating a prison at Stanford University. He assigned some of his subjects with the role of warden and others with that of prisoner. He and my father and their team watched in astonishment as the wardens—regular university students—committed barbaric and atrocious acts against the prisoners—their fellow classmates."

Daphne shifted nervously in her seat. "That was allowed?"

"Well, Zimbardo made the decision to end the experiment early, against my father's wishes." Hortense leaned forward on her messy desk. "It's unfortunate. We might have learned a great deal more."

At the expense of the subjects? Daphne wondered. She frowned. "So am I a lab rat?"

Hortense Gray narrowed her eyes. "I'm running an operation here that is guaranteed to make you glad to be alive. Although our resort is less than ten years old, I have been perfecting my techniques for my entire career. My success rate is impeccable. I give hope to family members with depressed and suicidal loved ones when no one else can. Currently, people see me as a last resort because they consider my methods…dubious. But one day, I will be the premier clinical psychologist, like my father was in his day. I'm already quite well-known in my field, though I wasn't always as successful with my patients as I am today."

Daphne listened to Hortense, but she was growing bored with all the self-praise, and her eyes couldn't avoid looking around the strange room at the different pieces of art and at the books packed onto the bookcases and stacked on the floors.

"You like my collection?"

"Hmm?" Daphne felt the color rush to her cheeks as she spun around to meet the doctor's curious gaze. "Yes. It's quite large."

"I know. I have a hard time parting with anything, even though I rarely read a book twice or look at a painting more than a few times. They're so dead, you know? So frozen…so…what's the word I'm looking for—unsatisfying—after a while, anyway."

Daphne couldn't relate to the doctor's words. She had never had a problem reading a book more than once.

"Life can get that way, Daphne. It can become stale, frozen, dead. We can get stuck, and sometimes it takes something truly profound to bring us back to life."

"So you scare the crap out of people to wake them up?"

"Not exactly, though terror is definitely an impetus for awakening one's soul. I prefer to think of my domain as living art, and a place where science and art come together. Here at this resort, you have the rare opportunity of stepping into a painting, or a musical composition, or a book and of bringing it to life as you resurrect your own stale, frozen, dead self."

Daphne didn't get what the doctor was trying to say, but she didn't like all this talk of death and resurrection. Truth be told, Hortense Gray sounded crazy, and Daphne just wanted the hell out. She would stay, though, because it was what her parents wanted.

"And Arturo Gomez knows what you're doing here at his resort? He's okay with it?"

Dr. Gray smiled and flapped a hand in Daphne's direction, like she was swatting a fly. "Arturo Gomez was one of my first patients. He adores me. I saved his life, and now he is my Ariel."

"Your what?"

"In *The Tempest*, Prospero, frees a spirit from a tree, where the spirit had been imprisoned by a witch for many years. The spirit, Ariel, made Prospero's domain possible. He gave him the magic Prospero needed to orchestrate his world. So, you see, Arturo, who is wealthy beyond imagination, is my Ariel. I freed him, and he gave me his magic."

Daphne nodded, thinking, *How nice for you both*, but kept her thoughts to herself.

Then Daphne gasped. As Dr. Gray removed her purple velvet jacket and laid it across one side of the desk, one of her arms, usually covered by long sleeves, was briefly exposed. Daphne caught sight of a number of scars, where long gashes must have once appeared. The doctor noticed and quickly pushed the wrinkled sleeve back down across her arm. Daphne wondered how the doctor got the scars but was too afraid to ask.

Hortense Gray cleared her throat and said, "I know more about you than you might have assumed, Daphne. I have a complete file on you. And there's something about your case, a piece of the puzzle I don't think you've noticed is missing."

Daphne felt her neck and back go limp and wobbly, so she grabbed the arms of her chair. She wasn't prepared to discuss her "case."

"According to my records, your brother, Joey, exhibited symptoms of paranoid schizophrenia by age sixteen and was diagnosed at age seventeen, but your parents opted not to put him on medication until much later. Is that correct?"

Daphne nodded, her mouth too dry to speak.

"And he was nineteen when he attacked and killed your sister, Kara."

Daphne waited. What was the doctor's point?

"Your mother shared with me what she said to you the morning she discovered Kara's body."

Daphne stared at the floor as sweat tickled the back of her neck and the inside of her palms. She wanted out.

"She thinks *she's* the reason you tried to take your life."

Daphne's mouth dropped open. She couldn't believe what the doctor was saying. Her mother blamed herself? "But that's not true."

"She made you feel like it was your fault."

"It was. You don't know the whole story." Daphne's heart pounded.

"But if your parents had gotten proper treatment for your brother…"

"Stop! It wasn't their fault!" Daphne stood from the chair. Why was the doctor saying such things? Was this part of her crazy therapy? Time to lie and blame others?

"So maybe this is about your need to believe in your parents?"

Daphne stared back at the doctor in shock. She heard a pounding in her head. "I don't know what you mean, but you don't know everything."

"Look at me, Daphne." Hortense Gray also stood. "Kara's death was not your fault."

But she was wrong. The doctor didn't know what had happened that night.

Again, Dr. Gray said, "Kara's death was not your fault."

Tears flooded Daphne's eyes and, since she couldn't speak, she ran from the room.

She heard Dr. Gray calling after her, but she took the stairs to the bottom floor and ran from the building. The other kids were still at the pool, most of them lying on loungers. She avoided them again, feeling numb and weak. As she reached the door, Cam appeared around the corner of her cabana.

"Daph?" His smile faded. "What's wrong?"

She ran inside and flung herself on her bed. "Nothing."

He followed her inside and closed the door.

"Aren't you supposed to stay away from me?" she asked accusingly.

He stretched out on the bed beside her, on his back. "I don't care. Talk to me."

"I'm tired of talking." She couldn't look at him, didn't want to look at another person again. She wanted to crawl into a hole and die.

He turned to her and wrapped his arms around her and held her, stroking her hair, not saying anything, until, at some point, she must have fallen asleep. When she awakened, entangled in arms and legs, in that twilight between sleep and wakefulness, she looked at the boy beside her, expecting to see Brock. Her heart skipped a beat when she saw it was Cam.

Then he awoke with a start. "What time is it?"

She glanced at the clock. "Eleven. Are you hungry for lunch?"

"I've got to go. Promise me you'll go horseback riding?"

"Is Bridget going?" she felt petty for asking, especially when she knew her heart still belonged to Brock.

He smiled and said, "No. She doesn't like horses."

"Okay then. Three o'clock?"

Cam nodded, before kissing the top of her head, and walked out the door.

Lying beside Daphne was the book Hortense had given her, *The Tempest*. She picked it up and carried it across the room to one of the striped chairs. The book fell open to a page that was marked with a folded piece of paper—a clipped, yellowed newspaper article:

May 1994: Harvard Professor Fired for Unethical Practices: New York: Dr. Hortense Gray, Harvard Professor of Psychology, was recently relieved of her duties by the Harvard School of Psychology when her paper, "Using Pain to Stimulate Pleasure in the Clinically Depressed," was submitted to and rejected by the American Journal of Psychology. *The paper was rejected because it revealed methods the journal and the university deemed unethical. According to Dr. Fordham, chair of the Department of Psychology, Dr. Gray administered pain treatments to subjects diagnosed with clinical depression in order to locate the point at which a subject's desire to die becomes replaced by the drive to survive. Dr. Gray hypothesized that when "the survival instinct kicks in, suicidal tendencies are overcome and the patient is cured"...*

The article went on to say that Hortense was the adopted daughter of renowned psychologist, Dr. Malcolm Gray. The article also mentioned that Hortense was one of many orphans adopted by the psychologist who himself had been accused but never charged of using the children in his own experiments.

He used orphans—his own daughter—in his experiments?

Daphne looked through the rest of the book to see if there was anything more, and when she found nothing else, wondered if she'd been meant to find the article, or if the doctor would be mortified to know Daphne had it. Daphne also thought again about the long scars all over the doctor's arms. Did her father's experiments have anything to do with them? A shiver skipped down her spine.

Then she opened *The Tempest* and began to read.

CHAPTER NINE

Runaway

Later that afternoon, a group of them met at the same sunny clearing near the jeeps, where they had met for the sunset cruise. Daphne and Emma climbed behind Roger and Cam. Daphne was relieved to learn Cam had been telling the truth about Bridget not coming, even though she had worn her yellow backless halter top and most flattering navy shorts just in case.

She hated herself for wanting Cam's attention, but there it was.

Another jeep—with the round-cheeked, older woman named Mary Ellen sitting beside Phillip in the front seat and with Dave and Vince in the back—followed Roger up the road and out of the canyon. They drove for five or ten minutes along the canyon ridge until they came to the Nature Conservancy headquarters. Cam told her that the oldest of the buildings, the chapel, constructed during the ranching period, had been converted into stables. Kelly, the guide, whom Daphne had briefly met at dinner her first night on the island, greeted them and gave them instructions before taking them into the pen and helping them to mount, one by one.

Daphne waited her turn next to Cam and Emma on the dirt with the sharp smell of animal and leather and hay. A gentle breeze made the smells bearable.

Kelly looked to be in her late thirties and was a redhead with green eyes. She wore jeans and a white tank with an unbuttoned denim shirt. When Kelly explained that she had just returned to work on the island after ten months of maternity leave, they all congratulated her on her baby.

Daphne rode a white mare named Pearl. Kelly led them on a gray gelding called Chief from the pen and up the canyon ridge toward the deep valley.

Kelly warned everyone not to let the horses feed on the tall grass along the hills. The riders should, instead, show them who was boss by forcing them on the trail. There wasn't a literal trail. She meant to keep the horses in line. But the horses didn't stay in line. They kept vying for the place behind Chief. Pearl bit the butt of the horse in front of her, and it kicked back, startling Phillip, its rider. Kelly apparently hadn't seen, and Phillip said nothing.

As they ascended the hill to the canyon ridge, Daphne felt a little nervous with the big animal moving beneath her. She hadn't ridden since she was nine, when her parents had taken her, Kara, and Joey on a family trip to Durango. Her mother wouldn't join them on the trail ride, saying she didn't like horses, but Daphne could tell even then that her mother was frightened of them. This had added to Daphne's own fear. She was frightened then, riding up and down the steep San Juan Mountains and through the national forest. And since Joey's horse had stayed near hers, he had been the one to keep her brave and cheerful.

Today, Cam was along to support her, but her fear was made worse by the anxiety she felt over anticipating the next exercise. She feared she was being set up for another terrifying experience. She wondered why she had agreed to come, if she were so uncertain; but she knew why: she was curious to see what would happen. Plus, it was so unlike her regular, dreary, gloomy life. And, most of all, her parents had wanted her to experience this.

From the top of the ridge, the view was spectacular, reminding Daphne of how she pictured the Shire in *The Hobbit*. Green grass grew down in the valley and along endless hills to either side—again making her think of a fairway—all the way down to the stream, which turned and curled like fancy, cursive penmanship. Mounds of shrubs in darker shades of green contrasted with the emerald color of the grass, and then whole bushes of yellow poppies and purple mountain glory added to the serenity of the view. The hills rolled low in areas, like hobbit barrows, and then became more jagged and rocky and taller further away, toward the mountains and their purple peaks on either side.

Kelly turned her body in the saddle, so she was facing the group behind her. "We're about to head down into Central Valley. This valley runs along a fault line dividing the northern half of the island from the southern. It also divides the two mountains, Mount Diablo to the north and Sierra Blanca to the south. A stream runs all the way through Central Valley from Prisoners Harbor, where you docked, to the west end at Black Point. You'll find a variety of wildlife throughout the valley, including the island fox, the island scrub jay, the Pacific tree frog, the bald eagle, the island deer mouse, and several plant species, such as morning glory, monkey flower, and buckwheat. Some plant species here are found nowhere else in the world."

The ascent was nothing compared to riding downhill. The hooves slipped on rocks, causing the horses to stumble, and this did not deter them from biting one another. Pearl ran forward and pushed her way behind Chief, causing Daphne to let out a little squeal of fear. She pulled back on the reins.

"Whoa, Pearl. Slow down."

"There you go," Kelly said. "Show her who's boss."

"Show her who's boss!" Dave was laughing. "That's classic! Show her who's boss!"

Daphne had no idea what Dave found funny.

Pearl kicked at Phillips's horse with her hind legs and then came down and reared back, nearly throwing Daphne off. Daphne's heart beat fast and she couldn't speak.

Kelly turned Chief around. "Whoa, Pearl! Whoa, girl!"

Daphne didn't think it did any good as she caught her breath and tried to slow down her heart. If the horses had at one time considered Kelly their leader, they no longer remembered it. She was like any other rider to them now.

Emma called out, "You okay, Daphne?"

"Yeah. I'm okay." Her heart still raced, and she couldn't breathe as she clutched the reins.

She glanced at Cam, who looked at her, white-faced.

"Sure?" he asked.

Daphne nodded, still breathless.

She followed Kelly and the Chief further into the valley.

After several yards, Kelly gave them more information about the area. "There are some other interesting plants, such as the native Jimsen Weed the Chumash used as a ceremonial hallucinogen, and the non-native African iceplants and European milk thistle. There's milk thistle over there," Kelly said, probably aware but not willing to acknowledge her lost authority over the horses.

The milk thistle resembled a medieval flail with its thick green stem topped with a green spiked head. A few purple blooms on its tip might have been blood.

"We'll take the horses down to the stream for a drink. They'll go right to it. You don't have to do a thing."

The horses scattered in a trot despite the commands of their riders, but when they reached the stream, they stopped and drank and seemed ready to submit again.

"Okay, everybody," Kelly said. "If you'll notice the leather pouches near your knees, you'll find plastic water bottles. Each rider has two: one for the ride out, and one for the ride in. If you'd like to dismount and taste the spring water, go right ahead. It's delicious."

Phillip and Emma climbed down and bent over the stream as Kelly continued to talk.

"From here, we'll follow the stream down further into the valley. Although there aren't many trees, keep your eye out for occasional low branches and use your reins to steer clear of them. I'll lead you to the top of Mount Diablo, which is on the northern side of the island and also the higher of the two mountains at 2,450 feet above sea level. On clear days, you can see the California coast from there, and at this time of year, there's a good chance we'll spot whales."

This solicited excitement among the riders. "Oh."

"Yay!" Emma said.

"I hope so!" Dave shouted in his rowdy voice. "We didn't see any the last time we came, did we Vince."

Vince shook his head in his usual mute way.

"How long is this trip, roundtrip?" Phillip asked.

"Two hours. It's roughly three miles to the base of the mountain and another mile to the top," Kelly replied.

"That water *is* delicious," Emma said as she climbed up in her saddle.

"Good," Kelly said. "Let's get started."

Kelly led them to a narrow part of the stream where the horses could easily jump across, but as soon as Pearl landed, she took off at a canter in front of Chief. Daphne pulled back on the reins, "Whoa! Whoa, Pearl!" Pearl reared back, again nearly throwing Daphne.

Kelly caught up to her. "Don't pull back so hard and so fast. You're going to get yourself bucked right off!"

"Sorry."

Kelly chastised Pearl, but again, Daphne doubted Pearl cared.

Daphne decided she did not like horseback riding. The lack of control over an almost wild beast beneath her was terrifying.

When the others caught up, Pearl maintained her place behind Chief and behaved herself. Cam was a few horses back, but Daphne wasn't about to make Pearl wait for him.

Up ahead to their left, toward Sierra Blanca to the south, smoke swirled up in great dark curls.

"What's that?" Daphne asked.

Kelly spoke loudly so the others further back could hear. "A contained fire. Don't worry. It's a standard procedure used by the Nature Conservancy. It restores nutrients to the ground and controls vigorous, non-native plant life, such as fennel."

"Non-native?" Phillip asked. "How did it get here?"

Kelly pulled up beside him. "From the ranchers who came after the missionaries shipped the Chumash off to the mainland. It took years to get all the pigs and sheep out of here. We're still working on the plant life."

Two wooden signs on a single wooden post jutted from the ground, and sitting upon it was a blue bird. "The scrub jay," Kelly pointed out. The bird looked at them and flew away.

The top sign read "Centinela."

"What does that mean?" Daphne asked.

"The Sentry," Kelly explained. "This is a crossroads leading three different ways."

"Ooohh!" Dave crooned. "Love it. Sounds like a character in a video game. Watch out for dragons." He laughed at his own joke, but no one else did.

The bottom sign pointed forward to Christy/West End, to the left to Ridge Road, and to the right to Diablo. Kelly led the group to the right.

"If we went straight, we would come to the western side of the island, where you would see the old Christy Ranch. It's also where most of the Chumash ruins and archaeological sites are located. No one is allowed on that side without a permit from the Nature Conservancy, not only because the sites are under its protection, but also because the western side of the island is more difficult to navigate."

"Some say it's haunted," Dave said.

"Yes, that's what they say," Kelly said. "Haunted Bridge divides the old Christy Ranch from the Chumash ruins, and people say they've seen and heard weird things."

"Have you?" Mary Ellen asked.

"I don't go to that side of the island."

"You don't actually believe the stories, though, do you?" Daphne asked.

"I don't know what to think of them, to tell you the truth."

After a while, Kelly resumed her guided tour speech. "If I would have led you to the left from the Centinela sign, toward Ridge Road, we would have crossed to the south to a place called Laguna Point, which is not far from the resort and just east of Sierra Blanca."

Gradually the terrain became steeper and rockier, and the sun blasted down on them without relief. Fingers of sweat ran down Daphne's neck and back and tickled her forehead. She reached into one of the two leather pouches and took several gulps from the water bottle, grateful when they climbed out of the valley and up into the wind.

Pearl jumped forward. Daphne turned. Phillip's horse bit and nudged Pearl's rump. Pearl kicked back but lost her footing and slid backward several feet. Daphne's breath caught as she held tightly to the reins.

Shoot, shoot, shoot. What the heck am I doing?

"Steady, girl." Her voice sounded soft and weak. "Steady," she said more loudly.

Phillip's horse took the position behind Chief, and before Pearl could maneuver herself behind it, a red mare moved in line, snorting at Pearl. Pearl fell in behind the red mare, biting and pushing. Daphne took the reins and steered Pearl out of line, hoping to get in behind Chief. They neared the top of the mountain, forming more of a clump than a line, so Daphne allowed Pearl to choose her spot as they gazed out at the great blue sea ahead of them.

"Wow," Phillip said.

"Hey, Daph." Cam moved beside her on his brown gelding. "What do you think?"

The magnificent view had an immediate calming effect. "It's beautiful. Absolutely gorgeous." She gave Cam a smile.

The wind cooled them beneath the sun's rays. Although clouds were gathering to the west, the northern skies remained starkly blue, as blue as the sea. To the east Daphne could make out along the gray horizon the shape of the California coastline—its lights, smoke, and highest buildings.

"Over there!" Kelly pointed. "I see a pair of humpbacks. Wait for it. You'll see them in a minute."

"Where?" Emma asked.

Everyone followed Kelly's finger.

"Just there. See them?"

Two giant whales rolled over the surface of the water, side by side. Then one leapt up into the air, spinning like a football before falling beneath the surface.

"Oh!"

"Wow!"

"Brilliant!"

The second whale also leapt behind the first, and then turned and lifted its tail to make a big splash toward the onlookers, as though putting on a show for them. The whale hit the water with its tail two more times.

Daphne couldn't believe how majestic they appeared and how close and visible they were. "Amazing!" she cried, forgetting everything else but the vision of the magnificent creatures in the sea. She wished she had brought her cell phone along so she could take a picture.

Phillip and Mary Ellen promised to get her email address later and send their photos to her.

After the whales were gone, the group made its descent with Kelly in the lead. Daphne failed to get Pearl behind Chief, and so she was anxious. Pearl bit and kicked and slipped on rocks. Daphne pulled her out of the line a few times. Now, Pearl ambled over to the right of the group and chomped on tall grass.

"Come on, Pearl," Daphne commanded, kicking the horse's side and gently tugging at the reins. "Come on. Let's go." The rest of the group continued down the mountain, apparently unaware they were leaving Daphne behind. "Go, Pearl!" Daphne kicked hard with desperation along the horse's sides, but instead of turning to follow the others, Pearl reared up and ran to the west, at full canter, down the steep slope of the mountain.

Crap. Where were the others? "Help! Help! This way!" Daphne screamed and hollered, but now, more importantly, she focused on staying on the horse. Pearl continued to run, slipping and sliding, and leaping over larger rocks. "Whoa! Oh my God!" She pulled back, to no avail.

Daphne could no longer hear herself screaming, but her throat burned, and her mouth was open. Tree branches scraped her arm and thigh as Pearl ran past, leaping over fallen logs and shrubs of poppies, and slowing only to evade large boulders. There weren't many trees on this island, but Pearl managed to assault her rider with them.

The terrain was rocky here, and hilly, unlike the smooth grass of Central Valley. Pearl slipped on a cluster of rocks, reared back, and though Daphne hugged the body of the horse with her legs and clung to the reins, she was thrown off onto the hard ground below.

"Pearl!"

The mare trotted off, past more boulders, and out of sight.

Daphne's bare back had taken the brunt of the fall, and as she tried to stand, she gasped with pain. Her left leg was also sore and cut. Against the painful protest of her body, she climbed onto the tallest rock and shouted, "I'm over here! Anybody? Can you hear me? I'm over here!"

Feeling dizzy, she sat on the boulder and tried to get her bearings. Which way was north? If only she had a compass. She sat for a few minutes, putting pressure on her wounded leg and hoping the others were already on their way. Surely, this was not a game. She could have died when she was thrown off that horse. Unlike the elevator and the cave, where she had company and was safe, being thrown and lost wasn't some new therapy doctors could control. This was an accident, plain and simple, and soon she would be found.

As she sat waiting for civilization to find her, Daphne thought of every terrible thing in her miserable life: Grandpa's death, Joey's sickness, Kara's death, Brock's sadness. Tears filled her eyes as she recalled the anguish that had crossed Brock's face when she told him she could never be happy. She should have gotten out of bed. Even now, it felt wrong to call it anything but her fault. She had killed Kara.

"Let's take a break," Brock had said when she could no longer look at him.

The black smoke curled into the sky in front of her and, remembering the contained fire was to the south, she hiked up onto a high rock and scanned her surroundings, now glad to have her bearings. She hollered out a few more times, hoping to be heard. Although she saw no sign of her party, she headed in the direction she thought they were most likely to be, in the direction of the smoke.

The hot sun beat down on her and reflected off the rocks. Wishing she had her water bottle, she licked her dry lips and limped on. The Central Valley should be up ahead, and there would be the stream.

It was slow moving over the rocky hills, and more than once Daphne lost her balance and slid on the loose gravel underfoot, as the horses had done. Each time she reached a hill, she expected to see the valley below, but every time, another hill emerged. She feared the black smoke must have blown west, leading her to the haunted side of the island.

"I don't believe in ghosts," she said aloud.

A flash of light cut through the sky, like the jagged blade of a sword. Up ahead, the dark clouds clustered, mixing with the smoke from the fire floating away in curled ribbons. Daphne wondered if she were making a mistake by moving from her spot. She should have stayed put. She glanced over her shoulder, thinking she should turn back.

Startled by a movement on the ground behind her, she froze. A moment later, it came again, but this time she saw the little animal. He must be an island fox. He was no bigger than a house cat with the snout of a terrier and the tail of a squirrel. Daphne's tensed muscles relaxed. She was glad to have his company.

"Hello there," she said.

She expected the fox to run off, but he didn't. Then she noticed the white tag on his tail and realized the Nature Conservancy was tracking him. Maybe he was used to humans. Daphne bent down, her back hurting, and said, "Hi, little fellow. How are you?" She put her hand low to the ground, but he wouldn't come to her; nor did he run away. He stood there, staring.

She turned and limped on, heading a little more to her left, which she thought must be south because of the clouds and the lightning. Every so often, she glanced over her shoulder and was pleased to see the fox was following her. She was on the verge of tears and frightened, but now not so lonely with her new friend.

Up ahead, a row of pines and a grassy valley stretched in the distance. She was disappointed she hadn't found Central Valley, but it was better than the endless rocks. The row of pines was thin and not high, and on the other side was a yellow patch of hay. Her back had loosened up since her fall and though her leg was bleeding, she could walk without limping. She hiked down to the grass and across the yellow field just as the rain began to fall. Two short oak trees in the distance seemed like her best bet for shelter. As she hunkered down beneath the limbs, she noticed the fox had followed, though he kept his distance.

"Come on," she said. "I won't bite. Will you?"

He didn't move. He stood in the rain.

"Suit yourself."

Daphne scoured the area from beneath the trees and tried not to be afraid. She still had several hours before nightfall, but what if she wasn't found by then? She sat in the grass against one of the thin trunks, crying a little and trying to think of what to do when she noticed, just past the yellow field of hay, an orange and gray dome tent.

She ran to it, and then hesitated in the rain, like the fox had. She weighed her options and when another thick blade of lightning cut through the sky, followed by the sharp whip of thunder, she ran for the tent.

The rain pummeled down, drenching her.

"Help!" she cried from the outside. "Please help me! I'm lost!"

The zipper was undone and out popped a head of dark curly hair. "Daphne?"

"Stan!"

CHAPTER TEN

Jimsen Weed

S tan held the tent open for Daphne to step inside. It was too small to stand upright, but not so small as to make her feel uncomfortable. She sat on the opposite end of his sleeping bag from him, shivering.

"What are you doing out here?" He handed her a towel. In his other hand, he held a funny-looking pipe, flat and made of polished wood. Smoke swirled up to the top of the tent where a few insects clung to the canvas.

She wiped her face and arms as she explained what had happened. The thunder rocked the ground.

"You were thrown? Are you hurt?"

She showed him her thigh. He handed her the pipe to hold while he took out a first aid kit and cleaned the wound with an alcohol pad. Then he found a scratch on her back, unprotected by her halter top, and cleaned it as well.

"I can't believe this happened. It's never happened before."

"What?" Daphne asked.

"I've ridden those horses. According to the guide, no one's ever been thrown before."

"I don't suppose you have any water."

He handed her a canteen. "Have as much as you like. I have more." He dabbed ointment on the open skin in both places. "I still can't believe this. You could have been killed."

She drank down several gulps. "Thanks." She gave him back the canteen and the pipe. "So what are you doing out here, besides smoking some strange-smelling stuff?" The smoke smelled a little like ginger.

"This? This is Jimsen Weed. The Chumash used to smoke it during their ceremonies. I'm going for an authentic experience." He smiled and took a puff from the pipe. Then he held it out to her. "Want some?"

"No thanks."

"I was hoping the rains would hold off until later this evening. I didn't get as much work done as I'd expected, so I was planning on staying one more night out here. But if the rain lets up before nightfall, I'll help you back."

"Thanks. I really appreciate it. I didn't know what I was going to do."

"This island's not that big. I'm sure they're searching for you. Maybe they'll find you and I won't have to take you. Not that I'd mind."

"I really appreciate it," she said again, feeling a little woozy from the smoke. She blinked hard.

"You don't need a drag off the pipe to feel the effects of the Jimsen Weed. There's enough smoke here to get you high. Do you feel it?"

"A little. I'm just tired. Sleepy."

"The Chumash used to smoke this and tell their stories about the ghosts of their women wandering the island. But this plant causes hallucinations. They were probably seeing things." He laughed.

"The horse guide seems to believe in ghosts, and Roger, the driver, does, too." Another crack of thunder made her jump. The rain beat at the tent, sounding like dozens of snare drums.

"They say weird shit happens on this side of the island."

"What kind of weird shit?"

"People see things. Strange lights and shadows. A woman in white. Figures chasing them. Once I thought something was chasing me, but it was nothing."

"Were you smoking then?" she teased.

Stan laughed again. "No, actually. But people also hear screams coming from Haunted Bridge." He told her more about the slave trader's wife, adding to what Roger had told her. "She didn't know what her husband had been up to. When she found out, she sank his ship before it could collect more slaves. Since then, lots of sunken boats in the area have been credited to her ghost."

She reminded herself that she didn't believe in ghosts. "I'm getting sleepy," Daphne said.

"Me, too. You okay?" He snuffed out the pipe.

Her lids felt heavy. "Okay. Relaxed." Her surroundings disappeared and there was only this one spot in front of her where her legs crossed. "A little sad."

"Sad?"

"I'm usually better at blocking out memories. I think I'm going to cry."

"Don't cry." He patted her shoulder. "Don't be sad. Shit happens, you know? Bad stuff happens to everyone."

"I miss Brock." Was there a bowling alley nearby?

"Who's Brock?"

"My old boyfriend. We were going to get married one day and open a private swim school. Is someone bowling?"

"No, that's thunder. I thought Cam was your boyfriend."

"Cam's my best friend. At least he was. I don't know anymore."

"What happened to Brock?"

"I wrecked everything. It was all my fault."

"We all make mistakes."

Daphne closed her eyes as the tears fell down her cheeks. She felt the need to write a poem. If she had her journal, she'd write:

You and I were meant to be
One another's destiny
But my mistake got in the way
And this is just another day.

"How are you doing?" Stan asked after a while.

"Sleepy."

"Let's take a nap. We'll sleep through the storm, and then, if it's still light, we'll head back." The thunder cracked again.

He unzipped the sleeping bag and unfolded it so it made a bigger mat for the two of them, and, side by side on their backs, they fell asleep.

Daphne is lying in her bed at her parents' house worried about her Advanced Placement World History Test. She's studied, but she's heard these tests are killers. She has just awakened from a dream in which she is taking the test and her pen runs out of ink, then her pencil lead breaks, and the tube of lipstick she uses bleeds all over the page, and soon she is bleeding all over the desk and floor of the classroom. The teacher glares at her and tells her to stop such nonsense. When she awakens, she lies in bed thinking of the test. Then she hears the thudding of Kara's headboard against the wall between their two rooms.

Maybe Kara is having a nightmare, she thinks. Or maybe Kara is doing sit ups because she feels guilty about the seconds she ate at supper. Maybe she is listening to her IPod and dancing on her bed.

Should she go check?

After several minutes, the thudding stops. Then she hears Joey walking in the hall. Is he going in or out of Kara's room?

Should she go check?

She rolls over and tries to sleep, worried about the history test.

In the morning, she's awakened by her mother's screams.

It takes her a minute to realize the screams are coming from Kara's room. She jumps from her bed to the room next door, and it is her turn to scream.

Kara is blue and dead.

Daphne opened her eyes to find Stan sitting up beside her in the orange and gray dome tent.

"You alright?"

She sat up and rubbed her eyes. She'd been crying.

"Must have been some dream," he said. "You were screaming."

"Sorry. How long have you been awake?"

"Not long. But look, the rain's barely coming down now. We might head back before dark, if you want."

"If you don't mind. How long was I asleep?"

"Couple hours. It's almost six. How's your leg?"

"Better. Got any water?"

"Here." He handed her a canteen.

The water was delicious. Daphne drank several gulps before handing it, half empty, back to Stan.

Outside the tent, they both heard a loud rustling.

"What the hell is that?" Stan whispered.

"A fox was following me earlier."

"That's too big for a fox."

The rustle came again, and twigs snapped. It sounded like a bear or a man. If it were her rescuers, wouldn't they be calling her name?

Stan poked his head out. Then he climbed to his feet and stepped from the tent.

"Stan?"

"What the hell?"

"Stan?" she poked her head out in time to see Stan run across the field hurdling over rocks past a structure of stacked stones and into a thick wood. She climbed out of the tent into the sprinkling rain. The little fox was a few yards away, but Stan was no longer in sight.

She hollered out his name a few more times, unsure whether she should search for him or wait in the tent. The fox showed the same indecision. As she was about to run across the field, she saw Stan running toward her, and he didn't look happy.

"What a sick bastard!" he shouted, diving into the tent.

Daphne rushed to his side. "What happened? Oh, my crap, your head is bleeding."

He had a gash across his forehead. He found a rag and applied it to the gash. "I saw a horse and rider, so I assumed he was part of your rescue team, but when I ran after him and got his attention, he charged at me."

"Why? Why would he do that?"

"Hell, if I know. Let's get out of here." He rolled up his sleeping bag and stuffed it into his backpack. He gathered other items and stuffed them in, too.

Daphne stopped. "Tell me the truth. Is this a game?"

"A game?"

"You know. A therapeutic exercise?"

"If this is, I'll be pissed. Someone will have some answering to do. You could have been killed. My head hurts like hell."

"So, you're really not in on it all?"

"I'm a grad student. An anthropologist. I don't know anything about any therapeutic or whatever."

She stared into his eyes, wanting to believe him. Maybe he was another patient, as Cam had said. "Do you think that man who attacked you is coming back?"

"I don't want to stay and find out."

"What about the tent?"

"It's easy to take down."

Stan slid the poles from the canvas loops and folded them with Daphne's help, though her hands were trembling so much she probably slowed him down. Stan rolled the tent around the poles and stuck it in a second bag, which he strapped onto the backpack.

"Let's get the hell out of here," he said.

CHAPTER ELEVEN

Christy Ranch

Daphne jogged behind Stan down a hill covered in grass and yellow asters in the sprinkling rain. Down below were two white buildings separated by a hundred yards. Near the smaller and closer of the two buildings was a deep ravine with a bridge stretched across it. Another fifty yards of flat land lay between the two buildings and the sea. The orange glow of the setting sun cast pinks and purples and oranges on the clouds above it and the waves below it.

"Aren't we going the wrong way?" Daphne asked. "We should be running away from the sun, not toward it. We should be going east."

"It's faster than climbing Sierra Blanca. We have to go around the mountain. There's a road up ahead by that bunkhouse." He pointed to the smaller of the two buildings, the one by the bridge.

As they neared the bunkhouse, Stan tumbled to the ground and hollered out.

Daphne bent over him. "You okay?"

He grabbed her hand and climbed to his feet, but then winced. "My ankle."

"Can you walk?"

He took a couple of steps forward, limping off the right ankle. "It's twisted."

She came up beside him and took his arm. "What'll we do?" She glanced around nervously for signs of the crazy rider. "Can you make it back to the resort?"

"I don't think I can hike that far tonight. We'll have to camp here, unless we get lucky and find someone from the Nature Conservancy with a jeep."

"But won't the crazy rider recognize our tent?"

"We'll have to hide in the bunkhouse. Can you carry my pack?"

His pack was huge and heavy, as heavy as the old television she once carried back into her bedroom when her parents upgraded the family tube. She helped Stan lift his arms free of it and had to rest it on the ground before slinging it onto her own shoulders.

"Shoot, Stan. What's in this thing?"

"Everything we need to survive, so be grateful," he said, half-teasing. "Take the pack down to the house. Then come back for me."

"What about the rider?"

"What are you waiting for? Go. I'll lie down and hide." He fell down into a pushup in the grass and flowers as Daphne took off down the hill.

So this is Haunted Bridge, she thought as she stashed the backpack near the house. The narrow bridge stretched forty feet across the ravine with wooden braces crisscrossing from its base. Pedestrians and horses only, she thought. A ladder in the middle of the bridge leading up from the deep crevice below seemed curious. She supposed there must have been spring water down there at one time. The wooden railings along the side were reinforced with a steel beam.

Running uphill, even without the pack, took more of Daphne's strength. She was breathing heavily by the time she reached Stan and helped him to his feet. Together, they made their way through the grass and yellow asters to the bunkhouse of Christy Ranch as the sun hovered, ready to set, in the distance.

The white paint was peeling off the old wooden door. Three two-by-fours were nailed across the front of it, but had come loose and hung useless, inches from the frame. The door stood ajar. Daphne was suspicious as they entered the old kitchen, feeling more and more certain she and Stan were being toyed with. Even if the rider weren't a deranged mad man, not knowing what would happen next filled her with anxiety.

The bunkhouse had a square table in the middle with two wooden chairs. A wood-burning stove against one wall was flanked by a sink and cabinets and an old white conventional stove. Further back were the frames for six bunks, three stacked on each side. Beyond the bunks, another doorway led to a screened porch facing the sea. On the opposite side was a bathroom. She opened the faucet, but no water came out. The commode was also empty. There was no sign of anyone else inside the house.

Stan sat on one of the two chairs as she retrieved the pack and brought it in.

"This door won't shut right," Daphne said.

"Put the pack on the floor in front of it. If anyone comes in the middle of the night, he'll trip over it and give us time to react."

"You're scaring me." She dropped the pack.

"I'm scaring myself. Can you get me that first aid kit?"

She found it and helped him clean up the gash and blood on his head as best she could with shaky hands, first with the alcohol pad, and then with the ointment. Now that she got a good look at it she found it was really more of a prick than a gash. "It's still bleeding. A Bandaid should do the trick." She found one in the kit, stealing glances through the two front dusty windows. "There. That should do it. It's not nearly as bad as I thought it was."

"Thanks. How's your leg."

"Fine. What about your ankle?"

"I don't think anything's broken. Wish I had some ice."

"You think we're safe here?"

"I think so, as long as he didn't see where we were headed."

She checked the corners of the screened back porch for signs of the rider and found instead a dusty old rocker. Lowering some of her weight into the chair, she tested it, and, when it held, relaxed into the old wood.

She studied the screened door off the porch and found it solidly board-ed shut with a barn door latch. "You can see the sunset from here. It's beautiful. Come on. It's a good distraction." She carried a chair from the table to the porch so Stan could join her. When she got him settled again, she asked, "Want some water?"

"Yeah. I've got several canteens in the pack."

She rummaged through his clothes and things and found them each a full canteen and returned to the rocker. "What'll we do if the rider returns?"

"Hide."

She looked at his anxious face. "It's probably just a game, an exercise. Don't worry. I don't think that rider really wants to kill us."

"I hope you're right."

They sat silently for a while sipping the water and watching the sun sink below the horizon. Gulls flew in front of the pastel-colored clouds. The rain dropped lightly, creating the illusion of invisible fairies dancing across the water.

Daphne had begun to like the resort and its experimental exercises until now. Allowing her to be thrown from a horse where she could have been seriously injured or killed was crossing the line. It was an accident, wasn't it? They couldn't have intended for her to be thrown. If they had, Daphne was ready to call it quits.

After twenty or so minutes had passed, Stan dug his pipe from his pocket and lit it. "This will make us feel better."

"You sure that's a good idea?"

"Best one I've had today."

Behind the bunkhouse, toward the bridge, rose a sharp scream.

Daphne stood. "What is that? Don't say a ghost. There has to be an explanation. The crazy rider?"

The sharp scream came again.

Stan puffed on his pipe. "Probably some kind of bird."

"That makes sense." Daphne got out the sleeping bag and laid it out on the floor between the bunk beds and noticed she was shaking. "Too bad these beds don't have box springs and mattresses."

"Too bad we don't have air conditioning and room service."

"Too bad we don't have cell coverage."

"Or beer."

"Or enchiladas. I'm hungry. Whatcha got in here?" She dug through the bag and found canned peanuts, beef jerky, and a tin of cookies. "I guess this will do." She grabbed his flashlight and returned with the food to the porch. She and Stan ate as they watched the colorful clouds turn to pewter and the horizon a pale strip of pink.

The scream came again.

"You sure that's a bird?"

"No. But what else could it be?"

"You don't believe in ghosts, do you?"

"Absolutely not. There's always an explanation for everything."

"Cam disagrees."

"Good thing he's not the one here with you." He gave her a flirta-tious wink.

He was cute, even with the bandaged forehead and unshaven face.

"Will you get me my lantern?" Stan asked.

Daphne found it in the pack and brought it to him. In a few minutes, he had it lit.

The smoke from his pipe permeated the air in the screened porch. Daphne thought about eating in the kitchen to avoid getting high from his secondhand smoke, but she liked sitting there staring out at the sea and sky as the sun sank and the moon and stars became visible. She also felt safer next to him. The breeze coming in through the screen wasn't heavy, but it did help circulate the hot air. Maybe she would move the sleeping bag in there for the night.

The scream came again, this time followed by a loud clatter.

Daphne jumped to her feet and crept to the front of the house to peer through one of the two grimy windows. A few feet away a small animal stood beside a fallen bucket. "It's the fox," she called to Stan. "He's been following me."

"I told you they're more like terriers than foxes. Cute, isn't he?"

Checking to make sure the rider wasn't around, she pushed the door open to get a closer view. The rain was barely falling now, more like a mist than a sprinkle. "Hey, boy. Whatcha doin' out here?" She took a few steps toward him.

The fox didn't move, but to her left, toward the bridge, she caught a blur of white. She turned to see a woman in a long white dress running away from her across the bridge. Daphne dashed through the house to the back screened porch to Stan. "I saw someone. A woman in white crossing the bridge."

"If you're trying to scare me, it's working." He put out the pipe.

"I'm serious."

The scream came again, but further away.

"It's the woman," Daphne said. "It must be their game. They're trying to scare us." It had to be a game, hadn't it? The woman couldn't really be an actual ghost. Daphne was no longer certain.

"Do you know how crazy that sounds?" he asked.

"Crazier than, 'There's a ghost out there'?"

A scratching sound came from the front door. Daphne turned to see a man with a white beard in one of the windows. *Oh my crap!* She moved closer to Stan. "There's someone out there. What do we do? I think he saw me." Her heart raced. She could barely think. They couldn't be ghosts, could they? Could the therapeutic games of the resort really reach this far, *go* this far?

"There's a gun in my pack. Front pocket. The one with the zipper."

Clearly, Stan didn't think they were ghosts, unless he thought you could kill them again with a gun. "I'm not going back to the kitchen."

"Then run for it. Follow the road back to the resort. Leave me here. Leave through this back door."

"No way." She peeked toward the kitchen and the front window. Then she sprang across the bunkhouse, over the opened sleeping bag, grabbed the pack, and dragged it back to the porch. She tried to unzip the pocket but couldn't grasp the zipper with her trembling fingers.

"Bring it here." Stan reached over and unzipped it, dug around, and pulled out the pistol. "Get behind me."

Daphne cowered behind Stan. Hairs stood on the back of her neck. Someone was coming. Something was out there. She shivered, waiting for the man in the window or the woman in white from the bridge. Then she worried Stan would shoot the gun. What if he shot an innocent person? If they were actors, they wouldn't know he had a gun.

The sun had set, but the moon and Stan's lantern kept the bunkhouse lit.

The scream came again, closer now.

"What exactly did you see?" Stan whispered.

"A woman in white on the bridge. A man at the window."

"Are you sure the island's legends aren't getting to you?"

"I didn't imagine them."

"The weed. It's made you see things."

"No. I know what I saw." But even now her eyelids felt heavy again and she wanted to go to sleep.

They stood there quietly listening, eyes on the front room.

When they heard nothing more, Stan said softly, "This reminds me of a time I went hunting with a buddy from undergrad. I wasn't much of a hunter. I'm still not. He talked me into going along. Anyway, we were out in a sorry excuse for a cabin after spending the early morning freezing our asses off in a blind. I was so tired. Dead dog tired. So we're getting ready to go to sleep when we hear something really strange. We didn't know what the hell it was. We were just like this: standing in the back corner, me with a gun. It was a rifle, but still."

"So what was it?"

"The damn refrigerator. There was this little unit in the back corner that would randomly start rattling. It took us a while to figure it out."

"But I saw the man with the beard. I know he was real."

After a few more minutes, Stan said, "Why don't you try to get some sleep while I keep watch? I'll wake you when I need to sleep."

"Don't shoot and ask questions later. This could be one of their games." Daphne pulled the sleeping bag onto the sun porch where Stan sat with his gun.

"Some game." He relit his pipe.

"I wish you wouldn't do that," she said.

"Just a few puffs to calm my nerves and then I'll put it out."

"Maybe I should take the first watch."

"Now you're starting to sound like my ex-wife."

"You were married?" Daphne lay down on the sleeping bag.

"For six months."

"What happened?"

"She decided she didn't want to be married anymore."

"You're still so young. You could marry again."

"Nah. I'm through with that gig. I like being on my own."

"Don't you get lonely?"

"Sometimes. You?"

Daphne shuddered. "Yeah. I feel lonely all the time."

"Even now?"

She glanced up at him and nodded, tears welling in her eyes.

He tapped his shoe to hers, a gentle nudge. "You won't always feel that way. You'll meet someone. Hell, you're the one who's still young."

"I miss my family." She meant her old family, when Kara was still alive, and Joey wasn't sick. In her mind she added, "And Brock."

"I'm sorry, kiddo."

She lay there watching the smoke swirl up to the cobwebs on the ceiling, clenching her jaw to keep back tears.

CHAPTER TWELVE

A Visitor

Sometime in the middle of the night, Daphne thought she heard Stan whisper her name, but when she lifted her head and turned to look at him, she found him snoring, his mouth hanging open with a bit of drool on his chin, the gun useless on the chair across from him. A lot of help he was. Keeping watch? Yeah, right.

Then she heard her name whispered again. "Daphne."

She sat up and looked around, but even in the dim light of the moon she could see there was no one else in the bunkhouse with them. Maybe she'd been dreaming. She lay back down close to Stan, but kept her eyes on the room around her, just in case.

"Daphne," the whisper came again.

"Who's there?" she said softly as she slowly sat back up. She waited for many minutes, sitting still as a statue, but, once again, she wondered if she might have imagined it. It might have been the wind brushing something against the house. She reached over Stan for the gun and held it in both hands as she lay back beside him, listening. She lay like that for a long time before she fell asleep.

Sometime later, the sound of a snort woke her. She opened her eyes and listened. She watched Stan, so when the snort came again, she knew it had not come from him.

She sat up.

The porch was in shadows this morning, though the bright sun shined hotly on the beach and water. There was no breeze, only a stiff heat that made her sweat even in her halter top and shorts. She had a funky taste in her mouth and her skin felt sticky. Something was moving on the side of the house. She could hear it through the screened porch.

"Stan," she whispered, shaking him.

When he didn't wake, she picked up the gun. "Stan, wake up."

"Not again," he complained.

"Huh?" she whispered. "What are you talking about?"

"All night long, I kept hearing you whisper my name, and then when I'd say 'what' you wouldn't answer."

Her skin went cold. "I never said a word last night." Could she have spoken in her sleep?

He narrowed his eyes at her.

The snort came again.

"Listen," she whispered, "There's someone outside."

He pulled himself to his feet, but stopped short, leaning on the chair. "My ankle."

Daphne frowned. "I'll go."

She got up and crept to the back door, still chilled by what Stan had said. She was suspicious of yet another exercise. Stan may not be in on it, but that didn't mean they weren't both being played by Hortense and her lot. Softly, she lifted both the hook and the two-by-for latching the door shut. The screen door creaked as she pushed it open. In the morning light, she could see another island across the ocean. Water from the storm clung to everything, including the pea gravel outside the screened porch. Out here there was a gentle breeze, and it lifted her hair as she stepped outside. She heard the snort just as she poked her head around the corner of the side of the house. Pulling up weeds with her reins hanging loose was Pearl.

So as not to scare the mare, Daphne quietly reached for a long tuft of grass and held it out. "Hi there, girl."

Pearl stared at Daphne suspiciously, but kept chewing. Daphne held her breath, sliding the pistol into her pocket to free the hand to reach for the reins. When the mare had pulled and eaten the last of the grass on the side of the house near the white picket fence, she inched toward Daphne.

"That's it, girl."

Before Daphne could get hold of the reins, Pearl flinched and trotted away.

Stan poked his head around the corner of the building.

"What was that?"

"Our ride back. At least it *was*. That's the horse that threw me."

"I'd rather walk than ride that horse, after the way it treated you yesterday."

Daphne put her hands on her hips. "You'd rather walk? On that ankle?"

Stan turned his back to her and hobbled for the back door. Before he reached it, he froze, still as a statue.

Alarmed, Daphne also froze and whispered, "What?"

She took out the pistol as she rounded the corner, doubting she would actually shoot it, but holding it gave her a sense of security. The white-bearded man from the night before stood in front of Stan, also frozen. His jeans were frayed at the hem with a hole at one knee. His t-shirt was filthy, the open flannel plaid shirt reeking of body odor. The white beard was matted and dirty, and his blue eyes were ringed by dark circles, though he wasn't old. Probably mid-fifties.

When he saw the gun, the bearded man put his hands in the air. "Don't shoot."

"You're the guy who attacked me yesterday!" Stan grabbed the gun from Daphne and pointed it at the bearded man. "Stay back."

"I barely touched you, man. I thought you were after *me*."

"Who are you?"

"Pete Coleman. A rancher from Arroyo Grande. I was a guest of the resort."

"Was?" Daphne asked, moving closer to Stan.

"Are you friends of Dr. Gray's?" the man asked.

Stan and Daphne glanced at one another, not sure how to respond.

"Sort of," Stan said. "Are you?"

"Not anymore."

"What are you doing out here?" Stan asked.

"A week ago, I came to the island by Dr. Gray's invitation. I was asked to participate in therapeutic exercises. If you'll put that gun down, I'll tell you the rest."

Stan pointed the pistol toward the ground. "Come inside and sit down."

Daphne brought another chair from the kitchen table onto the screened porch and all three sat down, Stan and Daphne on the opposite side of the room from smelly Pete.

"Tell us what you're doing here at the bunkhouse, Pete Coleman from Arroyo Grande," Stan said. "Now that you mention it, I think I've seen you around the resort."

"Why did you scare the crap out of me last night?" Daphne asked.

"I didn't mean to. I was coming back. This is where I've been hiding out the past few days. And I'm starving. Got any food?"

"Why did you leave?" Daphne asked.

Stan rummaged around in his pack and brought out a can of nuts and lobbed it across the room to Pete.

"Thanks," Pete said, cracking the lid and stuffing his mouth with a handful. "Those people are insane. As soon as I could, I grabbed me a horse and high-tailed it out of there. I've been trying to get off the island. The first two mornings, I rode out to Kinton Point just west of here hoping a boat would come, too scared to cross the island to some of the more popular points. I hung out at Kinton all day both days, until nightfall, starving to death, but no boat came. So yesterday I was desperate and tried for Scorpion Anchorage. I was almost spotted by that Cam guy who was snooping around on his horse with a couple of others, so I headed back here. When I saw your tent, I thought you were one of them, especially the way you came running after me. I nearly crapped my pants."

"Why are you scared of Cam?" Daphne asked. How could anybody be scared of Cam? He was harmless.

"Yeah. Why are you so desperate to get off the island?"

Pete gobbled more nuts. "I told you. Those people are insane. I came here because I met who I thought was a lovely woman. Turns out she's a freak like the others. The first night, a bunch of creepy women dressed like ghosts barged into my room and sprayed me with powder. The next day, during a hiking trip, supposedly to see indigenous plants, I was dropped into a hole and left in the dark with a bunch of mice and was rescued an hour later. The next day we went kayaking and were trapped by the tide in one of the caves, and my guide was attacked by a snake. I thought we was just having bad luck until that night we was dressed up in the ballroom and some terrorist types took us hostage at gun point. I suspected I was being toyed with, but I was terrified the whole thing was real. The next morning, the supposed terrorists surrendered to this team of naval officers and we were freed. But nobody can have that much bad luck. I told Dr. Gray I wanted to leave. She said I had to wait for her boat, and that it wouldn't come for another week. I decided I'd get the hell out of there as soon as I could, so the next morning, during our trail ride, I took off on that brown mare you saw me riding yesterday." He finished the last of the can. "Sorry. I ate 'em all."

"Where's the mare now?" Stan asked.

"Got her tied up over at the ranch house. I slept there last night since y'all moved in here."

"Was there anyone else with you?" Daphne asked, thinking of the woman in white she saw run across Haunted Bridge.

"I suppose you heard screams, too."

"We heard something," Stan said.

"I didn't just hear her," Pete Coleman said. "I saw her out on the bridge."

"Must have been an owl," Stan said.

Pete shook his head. "That was no owl. Could be the insane folks from the resort trying to torture me further, but it wasn't no owl."

"Why would they want to torture you?" Daphne asked, though she had her own suspicions. "What's the point?"

"Wish I knew. I couldn't help but think it's a weird form of entertainment for them, like a reality show, but in the flesh, you know? The owner, Arturo Gomez, spoke one evening about living art. I don't know."

Hortense Gray had also mentioned living art. What did that mean?

"You mean you think they're playing with us?" Daphne asked. "For their own pleasure?"

"I know it sounds crazy, but why else would they torment me?"

"As a form of therapy, like Dr. Gray said?"

"How can trauma be anything but psychologically damaging?" Pete asked.

"Well, they can't hold you against your will," Daphne said.

"They were, though. I didn't believe that crap about waiting for her boat. They weren't ever going to let me go."

Daphne thought of Emma's warning.

"Got any water?"

Stan handed over a canteen.

"Thanks." Pete swallowed down several gulps. "So what's your story?" he asked the two of them.

Daphne told how she had come to the resort with Cam to get away. She told about getting stuck in the elevator and trapped in a cave and attacked by sharks. When Daphne finished, Stan told how he'd come to study the Chumash ruins. He'd come before, back when there was no resort. Other than the elevator incident and the screams, he hadn't noticed anything strange or unusual during his stay, but he spent most of his time on this side of the island studying the ruins.

"Lucky you," Pete said. "But I wouldn't go back if I were you."

"All my stuff is still there," Daphne said. "My purse, my phone, and my best clothes."

"I've got a few things there, too," Stan added. "I've got all my notes here with me in my journal. I suppose I don't need the rest."

Daphne turned to Stan. "Are you thinking of leaving the island then?"

"What do you want to do?" Stan asked. "Go back to the resort?"

"I don't know." Surely Cam wouldn't let anything seriously bad happen to her—though being thrown by Pearl could have been deadly. What if he had lied to her and her parents hadn't really sent her there? "Do you really think Hortense Gray won't let you leave?"

Pete stood up. "I know she won't, and, unless you try to stop me, I'm heading over to Scorpion Anchorage again today. I think it's my only chance of getting off this island. You're welcome to come along. To tell you the truth, I wouldn't mind the company."

"He can't walk on his ankle."

"He can ride my horse. I wouldn't mind having an armed friend with food and water come along, even if I have to walk."

"What if we go with you as far as the outskirts of the resort?" Stan asked. "We can decide then whether we'll go with you to Scorpion Anchorage."

"I was planning on staying to the north, by way of Mount Diablo. I don't want to go anywhere near that resort."

"But that's where they'd be searching for me," Daphne said. "I'm sure they're all over that mountain."

"Yeah. Best to go around Sierra Blanca to the south. There's a road that will be easy on the horse, and there are a couple of harbors along the way, Morse Point and Punta Arena, where boats cruise with tourists to show them the sea lions and harbor seals."

"I don't know," Pete said. "I'd hate to be out in the open like that."

"There are plenty of bluffs and boulders for hiding. If we hear a jeep on the road, we hide."

Pete looked at Daphne and then back at Stan. "Damn. I guess it's better than doing it alone. Alright. We'll do this your way. I'll go get my horse."

Daphne followed Pete out the back door and watched him amble across the gravel, around the picket fence, and through the high grass toward Haunted Bridge. Gulls flew overhead, crying out above the sea, but none of them sounded like the screams from last night. A noise to her right caught her attention, and when she turned, she saw the little island fox that had followed her yesterday. He stood about ten yards away near the front of the house. She shielded her eyes from the sun and called out to him. "Good morning. It's nice to see a friendly face."

He stood staring at her and then took a few steps toward her. She squatted down and put an open hand on the wet ground. "Come on, then."

He stopped, sniffing the air.

"What are you doing out there?" Stan asked through the screened window without getting up from his chair.

"Saying hello to the fox. I also wanted to see if Pete really was doing what he'd said."

"You don't trust him?"

"I don't know."

The fox turned back and sat beneath a short scraggily tree. Daphne stood and scanned the bridge toward the ranch house. She felt sticky and stinky and wished she could take a shower and brush her teeth. She gazed back at the ocean, and its gentle lapping waves invited her. She needed to pee.

"I'm going to bathe in the ocean," she said. "Be right back."

She walked in her sneakers across the gravel to the sand, which was grassy in places, until she reached the pristine area washed smooth by the tides. Leaving her sneakers and socks on a rock, she walked in her bare feet, fully clothed, to the water, the sun warming her back. The cold water lapped over her feet, calming her. She decided the wind must have been playing tricks on her and Stan, but another part of her knew it was too unlikely that both of them would have heard their names whispered to them in the dark.

I don't believe in ghosts.

She looked toward the house, and seeing no sign of Pete and his horse, continued on till the gentle waves reached her waist. Then she knelt on the soft sand, pulled down her shorts and underwear, and relieved herself.

She strolled further out in the rolling waves. After a while as she rinsed her gritty arms and face, her memories of Joey and Kara at Santa Barbara Beach with their parents flooded her, and she stood, shaking them off, only to see Brock lifting her hair to kiss her shoulder, her neck. Daphne dived into the water and swam out to sea several yards, too deep to touch bottom. She turned on her back and floated, allowing the ocean to carry her back toward the shore, stealing glances back at the house for Pete and his horse. When she saw them coming across the bridge, she swam back and met them near the house.

"How was the water?" Pete asked.

"Nice. Clean. There wasn't a lot of seaweed or shells like I'd expected."

"I suppose I could use a dip myself."

Pete tied his horse to the white fence spanning the side of the house and followed Daphne into the bunkhouse, where Stan had already rolled up the sleeping bag and packed everything in his backpack.

"Ready then?" Stan asked when they entered.

"Ready as I'll ever be," Pete said. "Though, I never did get y'all's names."

They each introduced themselves. Then Stan took up his pack and hobbled to the mare where Pete helped him mount. With Pete holding the horse's lead and Daphne walking beside him wringing out her hair, they headed toward the south side of the island.

CHAPTER THIRTEEN

The Man at Punta Arena

As they walked up the hill from the bunkhouse toward the road, Daphne combed her long hair with her fingers, drying it in the gentle breeze, all the while looking about for people from the Purgatorium and wondering what her parents would think when they found out what was going on. At the top of the hill, the wind grew stronger, whipping her hair around her face. She fought with it until it was nearly dry, then she fastened the band in back to make a ponytail.

The road was not paved and was rocky and muddy and as wide as a single car lane. From the top of the hill, it leveled off onto a headland that dropped sharply to the water below. The wind was fierce on the headland, and the sky was cloudless. In a short while, Daphne's clothes were dry except for the thin padding of her strapless bra.

The water below was much more volatile on this side of the island, crashing against the bluffs with such force that Daphne was sure the ground was trembling beneath her feet. As high as they were, Sierra Blanca was still higher, blocking her view of the rest of the island, its grassy knolls and streams much different from this endless rock. Sparse, tall grass grew along the side of the road, occasionally tickling Daphne's arms and legs as it danced in the wind. There wasn't a tree in sight as they trudged a mile or so across the headland. Daphne felt her shoulders getting burned.

Kara would have enjoyed this hike. She had been shorter than Daphne, but more athletic and faster, even though she had cared more for music and dancing than sports. Daphne was the one who had partic-ipated in sports all through school, and she used to get frustrated, when Kara played with her, at how unevenly they were matched despite Daphne's hard work. But both girls had loved the outdoors, unlike their mother, especially when they went fishing, because that's when their father was the most talkative and the most relaxed around Joey and his growing antisocial behavior.

Once they were out on their pontoon boat at Inks Lake, all but their mother. Joey, fifteen, sat quietly, as he had been doing lately, slumped on the sofa seat.

"Don't you wanna fish?" their dad asked him.

Joey didn't reply.

Daphne punched his shoulder. She would have been twelve or thir-teen. "Fish with us. Let's see who can catch the first one."

"What's the point?" he asked. Then he whispered over and over, "What's the point? What's the point? What's the point?"

"Just for fun," said nine-year-old Kara. "It's better than sitting there."

"That's alright," their dad said. "Sit there and enjoy the lake."

Her mother didn't usually go along because she wasn't the outdoorsy type and because she was busy. Although she didn't work, she was in-volved in activities that kept her stressed and uptight. She was a board member of their homeowner's association, led a book club, volunteered as a mentor at the elementary school, belonged to a Bunco club, and, when Kara was still alive, studied to become a master gardener. She could be the most giving person in the world. The gifts at Christmas were over the top, and there were often little surprises waiting for all three kids on their beds when they got home from school, like a new book, or a poster, or brand-new markers. In spite of her tendency to be giving and loving, Daphne's mother spoke out in anger without think-ing, always regretting her words and making apologies, but the stinger of her words penetrated Daphne's skin and could not be removed.

She should have gotten out of bed that night she heard the banging when Joey went to Kara's room. He couldn't help himself. It was Daphne's fault. She gazed at the ocean, full of longing and regret over a mistake she couldn't undo no matter how badly she wished it. She could sail through the air and into the sea right now and end her agony.

Daphne stared longingly at the ocean and might have made a run for it had Stan not spoken.

"Damn, it's hot."

Daphne was shivering, cold as ice.

The road turned down the headland toward a gravelly beach below. As they descended, the sun moved in front of them. Behind her, up on the headland, was the little island fox.

Pete said, "I have a daughter about your age."

"Really?"

"Yeah. Stephanie. She's eighteen."

"I will be, in August."

"My son's twenty-five, but I never see him. He lives with his new wife in Costa Rica. They have a baby girl I've never met."

"Why don't you visit them?"

He held out one hand and then dropped it to his side. "I will. Some day."

"Why not as soon as possible?"

"Oh, it's complicated. My son doesn't want to see me."

Daphne crossed her arms at her chest and, without thinking, asked, "What happened?"

"To make a long story short, his mother died, and he doesn't want me to go on with my life."

"Maybe he just needs time."

"Maybe." Then he asked, "You get along with your parents?"

Daphne sucked in her lips and nodded.

"You tell them you love them?"

She shrugged. "It's been a while."

"How come?"

"I don't know."

"That's too bad. Life's short and goes by fast."

They'd been walking for what seemed like an hour when Stan lifted his finger toward the sea and said, "That's Morse Point over there, but I don't see any boats. Why don't we go on down to Punta Arena and eat? We can talk about what we want to do from there since it's about half-way to the resort."

As they continued their descent in silence, Daphne was unwillingly immersed in images of Brock—Brock blowing her kisses from across the pool, Brock swimming his magnificent butterfly, Brock playing chess with Joey, Brock begging her to please get help. Daphne loved him. As soon as she saw him, she loved him.

She now saw him, weary-eyed and frowning. "Maybe we need a break."

A swarm of butterflies lifted from the morning glory and into the air around Daphne.

"There's someone down there on the beach," Pete said, stopping the horse. "A man."

Stan dug through his pack and found a pair of binoculars. He pointed them toward Punta Arena. "I've seen that man before. He works for the resort."

"Let me see." Daphne took the binoculars from Stan. The man below was pulling a kayak onto the beach, his oversized bathing suit hanging low over his fleshy, bulky form. A long ponytail whipped in the wind. "That's Larry." *Hairy Larry.*

"What's he doing?" Pete asked.

Daphne handed him the binoculars.

"He's alone," Pete said. "Thank God there are no others."

"But they could be close by," Daphne said. "Searching for me."

"And me," Pete said.

"Let's sneak up on him," Daphne suggested. "Maybe we can get information out of him."

"I think we should avoid him," Stan said. "Continue around from up here and catch the road at the next point."

"But he might have answers for us," Daphne said. "We could use your gun to make him talk and tell us what the heck's going on. I need to get my things. My purse has all my money and my ID. How can I get home without it? But I'm scared to death to go back there. I want to know what Cam and Dr. Gray and the others are really up to."

"I agree," Pete said. "If nothing else, we could take his kayak and one of us could go to the mainland for help."

"No way anyone's getting to the mainland in a kayak," Stan said. "The waves are too strong to make it that far. You could get lost at sea."

"Or come upon a boat," Pete said. "I'm willing to take my chances."

"Come on, Stan," Daphne said. "Pete's right. This could be a chance for us to get help."

"I hear you, kiddo, but I don't think I can do much sneaking with a bum ankle."

"I'll go alone," Pete said. "Give me the gun."

"That's not happening," Stan said. "No offense. I don't know you."

"I'll go. You trust *me*, don't you?"

"If he wrestles that gun away from you, kiddo, we're screwed," Stan said.

"I won't let him get close enough. Come on. I can do this."

"We'll be right behind her, man."

"I have a bad feeling about this." Stan took the pistol from his pack and handed it over to Daphne.

"Is the safety on?" she asked.

He showed her how to turn it off if she needed to, a button right by the trigger, like the reverse button on her dad's drill. "But for God's sake, don't turn it off unless you're absolutely sure you can shoot it."

"Got it."

Pete led the horse behind a large boulder to wait while Daphne crept down the hill alone. She carried the pistol in her shorts pocket so as not to alarm Larry if he happened to see her coming. She had never felt so singularly focused. She wasn't a soldier going into battle, but it occurred to her this is what it felt like as the adrenaline pumped through her and she floated slightly above her own body. The earth could have trembled, a tidal wave could be threatening in the distance, and the only thing she would see was the man she knew as Larry on the beach of Punta Arena.

She was about twenty yards away when he spotted her and waved.

"Over here!" he shouted. When she got closer, he said, "Man, has everyone been worried about you."

She took out the gun and pointed it at him, hands trembling so much more than she had anticipated. "Wait right there."

"What? What are you doing? Where did you get that gun?" He came toward her.

She took a few steps back. "I'm not alone." She called out for Stan and Pete, and they showed themselves. "Let's go. You first."

Stan had dismounted by the time Daphne and Larry reached him near the boulder. Daphne was glad to be rid of the gun when she handed it back to Stan and let him do the talking. She'd never felt so much power over another individual, and she did not like it, afraid she could be responsible for another tragedy like Kara's. She took a deep breath and tried to shake off the nervousness.

"What's going on, Stan?" Larry asked. "Why are you doing this?"

"Nothing's going to happen to you as long as you answer a few questions. Sit down."

There were a few smaller boulders beside the larger, and Larry sat on one. "What questions?"

"We want to know what's going on back at the resort," Pete said.

"Yeah," Daphne chimed in. "Is this really about therapy? And can we leave when we want?"

"I don't know what you're talking about," Larry said.

"Don't pretend like we were stuck in that cave by accident," Daphne said. "Cam has already told me it was a set up. What was the point? To get me to face my fears?"

"I didn't like being in that dark hole with the mice," Pete said. "That was cruel and unusual punishment and grounds for a lawsuit if you ask me. And those terrorist types? You folks crazy?"

"Look, I don't call the shots, and I'll lose my job if anyone finds out I talked to you."

"What exactly is your job?" Stan asked.

"I give the cave tours, buddy. You know that." Larry got up. "And you and I both know you aren't going to shoot me, so I'm outta here."

Larry turned for the beach, but Pete tackled him to the rocky ground. "You son of a gun better start talking, or I'll beat the living daylights out of you."

Stan pointed the gun at Pete. "Enough. Get off him."

The two men pushed each other and sat on the rocks glaring at Stan.

"You guys got this all wrong," Larry whispered, rubbing his sore elbows. "The therapy isn't for you. It's for them."

Daphne leaned in. "Who?"

"The paying customers. The watchers."

"Who are they?" Pete asked. "You mean Dr. Gray?"

"No, no, no. You still don't get it. Dr. Gray is the master of her domain. She uses the word improvisation. Living art. She talks about the catharsis of tragedy. But it's not for you. You're the actors, but in a way, you write the script. The therapy is for the watchers."

"Are they watching us now?" Daphne asked. She followed Larry's gaze. His eyes rested on the island fox a few yards away.

"There," Larry said.

"The fox?" Daphne asked.

"There's a GPS chip and digital camera on his tail. He's been trained to follow you."

"You gotta get us outta here," Pete said, jumping to his feet. "I didn't sign up to be tortured for the pleasure of others."

"You can run, but you can't hide on this island," Larry said. "Just ask Stan here. He knows."

CHAPTER FOURTEEN

Escape at Laguna Harbor

What are you playing at?" Stan asked Larry.

Daphne and Pete both stepped back and stared at Stan in disbelief. Daphne's knees felt weak as she shifted her weight from one foot to the other.

"Hortense wants them brought back," Larry said.

Daphne searched Stan's eyes and was horrified by what she saw. Admission.

"Sorry, kiddo."

"How could you? Why?"

"It's not why, but what."

Pete took off running toward the beach, a wall of dust rising on the hillside. "I'll send help, Daphne!"

Larry followed but couldn't catch him. Pete reached the kayak and ran with it as far as he could before paddling to the east and out of sight.

"He won't get very far," Stan said.

Daphne pivoted and ran in the opposite direction of Pete, back toward the center of the island. Stan caught up to her before she reached the base of Sierra Blanca.

"You never hurt your ankle!" She gasped for breath and struggled to free her arm from his grip, but he held on. "It was a lie, like everything else." She hit his chest and slapped at his face, but he wouldn't let go.

"Not everything was a lie."

"I'll never believe another word you say, whoever you are!" She hit him once more before he put the gun away and pinned both arms at her sides.

"That's too bad. I hope you'll change your mind."

He pulled her back to the horse and to Larry, who stood hunched over, catching his breath.

"Please let me go." Her voice was soft. She stopped struggling. "I just want to go home."

A flock of gulls cried out above them and then disappeared beyond Sierra Blanca.

"Sorry, kiddo." He hooked his arm through hers, gripping her forearm, and walked her down the road, toward the beach, while Larry led the horse behind them. "That's not an option."

"Why? Can't you tell me what you're going to do with me?"

"I know this won't make sense to you now, but, ultimately, *you'll* decide."

"Whatever. Is your name even Stan?" Tears formed in her eyes.

"Yes. Yes, it is."

They hiked the serpentine trail, turning away from the beach and onto a ridge overlooking a lagoon. Daphne glanced back to see the island fox was still following them. She stuck out her tongue, not to the fox, which was as innocent as she, but to the watchers—Hortense and her lot—or whoever else might see. To make sure she was understood, she raised her free hand and shot the finger.

Larry chuckled behind her, making Daphne grit her teeth.

"I'm hungry and thirsty," she said after a while.

Stan said. "There's a little cave down at Laguna Harbor. We can rest there and eat."

"Then what?"

"It's about another half hour to the resort from there."

They followed the road down a steep incline towards a lagoon, passing an old wooden sign that read "Laguna Harbor." Here there was little sand compared to the beach at Punta Arena, mostly boulders and gravel along the shoreline, and one stretch of rock that formed jetties on the eastern side. The road then turned sharply back toward the north, up a steep hill, toward the center of the island, along a stream pouring into the lagoon from a five-foot drop. Larry led the horse to the stream above the falls for a drink, while Stan pointed the gun at Daphne and ordered her to refill the three canteens. Daphne complied, thinking only of escape.

Once the canteens were filled and the horse content, Stan led the party down the rocky embankment from the road toward the lagoon to a cave nestled behind the falls.

"Isn't this a pretty place?" Stan spoke loudly to be heard over the sound of the falls as he took two of the canteens and handed one to Larry.

Daphne drank the cold water without giving Stan the satisfaction of a reply.

"One of my favorites." Larry let the reins drop. He then found a rock to sit on inside the cave.

Stan dragged his pack into the cave and rummaged through it for food. The gun was near him on the ground and both hands deep in the pack. Daphne was hungry but worried this might be her only chance. She dropped her canteen and jumped onto the horse.

Larry tried to climb to his feet, but fell over like a crab on its back, arms and legs swinging. "Ah!"

Stan leapt from the pack and grabbed Daphne's leg, but she kicked and kicked till it was loose and then caught him with her shoe beneath his chin. Stan yelled and bent over, clutching his jaw as Daphne dug the stirrups into the horse and cried, "Go! Giddyup!" She slapped the reins and dug the stirrups, and the horse took off. Stan chased her, calling out commands to the horse. She kept the horse at a run up Sierra Blanca until the terrain got steep. She could no longer see or hear Stan.

"Good boy," Daphne said, petting his mane. "Thank you!"

She knew she would be a sitting duck at the top of the mountain, so she took the horse down to the east along the base hoping to find Central Valley, which she would cross to Prisoners Harbor to get help. The base of the mountain became difficult to navigate, because huge slabs of white granite jetted out of the ground, but as terrified as she was of the beast moving beneath her, she was even more frightened of Stan and Larry. She couldn't find a trail and kept stopping, turning back, and stopping again. She knew she couldn't turn back the way she had come, so she plowed onward, but it was taking a long time to get anywhere.

The sun shined down, hot and unrelenting, burning her skin. The salty sweat dripping down her face and chest stung. The drink from earlier seemed to have little effect on her thirst and only made her hungrier for something to eat.

She couldn't believe Stan had betrayed her. She had grown so fond of him in the short time they had spent together, but obviously she was no good judge of character. Hadn't Cam told her Stan was a patient? So either Cam had been lied to or he had lied to her.

Of course, he had lied. Her mother never would have sent her into such danger. This whole place was crazy and the sooner she could get off the island the better.

But she'd known Cam her whole life. He was her friend. How could he do this to her?

What had Larry meant when he said the therapy was for the watchers? She imagined she must be like a character in a reality TV show to them as they watched her fighting for her life. From where were they watching? And who were they? Or was this more nonsense meant to confuse her about the true purposes of the island?

When she cleared the granite spikes, she came upon a stream and decided to follow it down to what she hoped was Central Valley. Too frightened to dismount for a drink, she kept the horse at a walk, fearing she might be headed for an ambush, and began to wonder if she wouldn't be better off on foot so she could more easily hide in the brush and boulders. She lacked the horsemanship to outmaneuver any who might spot her. Plus, she was frightened of getting bucked off again.

Before she could decide what to do, she heard voices calling out ahead of her. Crap! She turned the horse back toward Sierra Blanca and made a run for it. The granite spikes slowed the horse down at first, but then she turned up the mountain, and soon they were flying toward the top. Despite the fear and adrenaline pulsing through her, her mind was clear. She commanded herself to think and act because she had no one else to depend on but herself. In answer to this command, she decided she would use the horse to get a head start, and then she would send him off, down the mountain, and hopefully they, whoever they were, would follow.

She found a cliff edge shrouded in dense brush with footholds up the steep side. She pulled the reins and stopped the horse, dismounted, and sent him running back down toward the stream. When the horse was out of sight, presumably headed toward Central Valley, she climbed up the steep cliff edge to the top to hide.

She wedged herself into the dense foliage at the top of the cliff, thankful to have shade, as the sun was at high noon and bearing down hot. Although she was only halfway up the mountain, this spot afforded her a clear view down the east and south sides of Sierra Blanca, all the way to the stream, where she had heard the voices, and to the south, almost to Laguna Harbor. If any approached from this side, she would see them. If any came from the west or the north, she would likely hear them.

As she lay in her nest, clenching the thin, smooth branch of whatever bush was shading her, she wondered again about Stan and how easily he had deceived her, but before she could think too long, a party ascended the mountain from the east—probably the source of the voices she had heard by the stream. She stiffened and held her breath, listening.

"You think she rode up the mountain?" The voice belonged to Cam.

"Only one way to find out," another man, maybe Phillip, said.

So sending the horse without her hadn't worked.

"Over there!" Cam said.

She lifted her head. Larry and Stan made their way up the mountain. They didn't seem to be in a hurry. Phillip and Cam were both astride horses. She ducked down when Stan and Larry reached the cliff edge below her.

"We lost her," Stan said.

"How?" asked Cam.

"We underestimated her," Larry said. "*We*, not just *me*."

"Phillip and I'll go to the top and look around. Why don't you guys head back and rest."

"I won't argue with you," Stan said. "She kicked the shit out of my jaw, and I've got a bloody damn headache now."

Daphne listened to the horses climb the steep edge to the west of her as Larry and Stan descended to the east. She lay there, not breathing, waiting. When she could no longer hear the horses or see the men on foot, she took a deep breath and let her body relax.

Then she noticed a trail of tiny red ants crawling along her hand and arm. Without moving the one arm, she swept her hand along the trail on her skin, killing the insects in one sweep. She released the branch, seeing it was infested, but not without receiving two painful stings on the back of her hand. She wouldn't be able to hide here after all.

She scrambled out of the brush and scanned her surroundings, wondering how to proceed. If she followed Cam and Phillip, it would be harder to get away if discovered. If she climbed down, she would be going closer to Stan and Larry, who could be waiting to ambush her. Their speech about returning to the resort might have been a ploy to cull her out of hiding. She skirted along the cliff edge, weighing her options, wishing she could find a cave to hide in until dark, but not sure if one could be found on Sierra Blanca. If it did have a cave, the others would know of it, and that's exactly where they would look. No, she needed to go down, down into Central Valley and head for Prisoners

Harbor without being seen or heard. She crouched low, behind the rocks along the mountain, heading for the spikes of granite when she spotted the fox a few yards away, staring at her.

Great. Just what I need.

If he continued to follow her, they would always know her position. She had to do something. She hated to take his life, but that seemed like the only way to save her own.

Maybe she could disable the tracking device on his tail without killing him. She crouched behind a boulder and collected a pile of rocks, the size of lemons, and waited for the fox to get closer. When he was about three yards away, she grabbed the biggest one in the pile and flung it like a baseball toward his tail, expecting to miss. The rock hit the fox right at the tail-head, and he flinched and stammered a few feet back. She wondered why he didn't run off. She took another rock and threw. This time she did miss. She threw again and again, causing the fox to dance as it evaded the rocks. She had two stones the size of ping pong balls left in her pile. She threw one right after the other, and the second one hit the fox on the side of the head. He faltered to the ground as tears poured down her cheeks.

I'm so sorry! Then, inexplicably, she looked at the fox and cried out, "Kara!"

Glancing in all directions, Daphne moved quickly toward the fox. She cradled him in her arms. "I'm so sorry," she whispered. She found the tracking device and twisted, but it wouldn't come loose from the tail. The fox was breathing rapidly and was frozen stiff, as she had been on the cliff under the brush moments ago.

She was sobbing now, sobbing uncontrollably and as hard as she had ever sobbed before. "I'm so sorry, little fella." She found a rock, one she had thrown, and, flattening his tail against the rocky ground, she used it to crush the tracking device. The fox winced as the rock struck his tail, but she hit it several times to be sure. Then, as quickly as she could, she carried the fox and ran toward Central Valley before the watchers found their way to the base of Sierra Blanca.

CHAPTER FIFTEEN

Danger in Central Valley

Daphne found a shady place near the stream and left the fox, praying he would be okay. Then she followed the stream to Central Valley. Luckily, as she moved to the interior of the island, away from rock toward grassy fields with small trees and shrubs, she found better places to hide. She was anxious to get to Prisoners Harbor but willing to take her time so as to not get caught.

She knelt over the stream beneath a shade tree and scooped up handfuls of water, saying a silent prayer for the fox and wondering if she should have kept him with her. The fear that she hadn't successfully destroyed the tracking device kept her from running back for him.

The fresh spring water tasted so good, she couldn't get enough of it. She allowed it to run down the front of her shirt, splashed some on her cheeks and the top of her head, but avoided getting her shoes and shorts wet, not wanting blisters or chaffing. Now that she was cool and her thirst had been quenched, she realized how exhausted she was. She decided to crawl into a thicket beneath a tree, a few yards from the stream, and rest. Checking for ants and other stinging insects and finding none, she hunkered in on her bottom, stretched out her legs in front of her, and leaned against the tree. Stan and Larry were ahead of her to the east, toward the resort, and Cam and Phillip would likely not double back, but would continue down Sierra Blanca to the north or west. Even if someone did pass through here, she was nicely covered. She closed her eyes.

As tired as she was, she could not sleep. She lay there thinking on the night she heard Joey in Kara's room, the night he killed her. He later said he was choking a demon from her body, trying to save, not kill, her. The banging of Kara's headboard as Joey strangled her and the pounding of the rock against the fox's tail thudded in Daphne's head, over and over, until she was sobbing again. The grief and regret Joey had expressed when he'd realized what he had done equaled to that shown on the day he had accidentally electrocuted their grandfather, except this time he went catatonic for three days. If only Daphne had gotten out of bed and had gone to check on the noise, she could have spared him that pain and saved her sister.

It occurred to Daphne now as she sat within the brush that she could easily take her life there in the stream. What was stopping her? Why go to all this trouble to be rescued if she didn't care to live?

Did she care to live? She wasn't as sure of her plan anymore, but she dismissed her doubts, believing she was just tired, hungry, and weak. She told herself that if she weren't on the run, she wouldn't hesitate to see her plan to the finish.

She scrambled from the thicket and followed the stream to where it pooled more deeply between two knolls covered in purple morning glory. A swarm of butterflies rushed from the flowers as she marched past. She tiptoed into the icy stream to the middle where it deepened to her knees and lay down, prone, submerging her face.

The water was clear when she opened her eyes, green moss visible on white rocks, and a few plants tilted and danced wildly with the flow. So that was what was meant by "going with the flow," she thought, as she held her breath. A turtle darted past, and she flinched, not expecting to see him there so close to her. She lifted her head from the water for a breath and returned underwater to try again.

This way the pain would be brief. If she had surrendered to Stan and Cam, who knows what other terrifying games and torture she must endure. This way, she had control over when and how. Her parents would be sad, but they were already so sad, and she wasn't convinced her death would add much more misery to their lives. At least they wouldn't have to look at her.

And Brock could go on with his life, if he hadn't already.

She sputtered when water got in her mouth and into her lungs. She lifted her head for air, trying not to cough, and submerged again.

This is it. No more air, Daphne. Just let it burn.

Her lungs did burn and, beneath the water, she coughed, and more water entered her lungs. She fought to hold her head under and tried to find pleasure in the burn, imagined the end, the nothingness, which was better than a life where she would continue to see the pain of her family, tried to embrace the burn and the sharp pain emerging around her eyes, hoping there was no eternity, just nothing, but it was too easy to come up and give in to the urge to cough and breathe.

She coughed and gagged, her throat burning as she glanced around, hoping she wouldn't be heard.

A gull overhead cried out and startled her.

This wasn't as easy as she had hoped. Maybe she should fling herself off a cliff. But when she imagined her body hitting hard against the crashing waves, being thrust against the sharp rocks, bones crunching and skin being split open, she cringed. No, drowning was definitely better than jumping.

She knelt there in the cold water and shivered. The sun was arching over to the west now, meaning it was past noon. Her stomach growled, but she felt nauseous and very tired. Too bad she couldn't simply lie in the water and fall asleep. She decided to turn the other way, to lie back in the stream and simply go to sleep. Then she recalled the painting in Dr. Gray's office and her heart stopped.

Daphne was the lady in the painting.

No, that was crazy. A coincidence. She sat on her knees, catching her breath, waiting for the dizziness to subside. Daphne was the lady in the painting, the painting brought to life. That couldn't have been planned.

Dr. Gray wasn't *really* like Prospero, capable of such magic. Was Daphne meant to be lost on this strange island just like Ferdinand in Shakespeare's play?

If this was all just one big ruse to get Daphne to want to live, it was failing miserably, for she had just tried to kill herself. She climbed to her feet, angrily shouting to the air around her, "Did you see that, Dr. Gray? You've failed! I'm no gladder to be alive than I was before I got to this God-forsaken place! Get that? You failed!"

She fell to her knees, trembling and wondering what the heck she had just done. Had anyone heard her? What would they do if they found her?

The sound of a jeep in the distance caused her to lift her head and scan the valley, and that's when she realized she was kneeling in the very place she had seen the two actors—the man pulling the hair of the girl the morning she had arrived. This meant the road was about twenty yards away. She swam down the stream toward a group of tall reeds and waited. She heard the jeep stop.

"This has gotten out of hand, guys." It was Hortense Gray. "Tell me again where she was last spotted."

"The base of Sierra Blanca." This sounded like Roger.

"If we don't find her, it will be the end of us," the doctor said. "When the rest arrive, organize a grid and search every inch. I want her found today."

"We'll find her." This was definitely Stan. "She's around here somewhere. Between here and Prisoners Harbor, no doubt."

"Don't say anything we wouldn't want her to overhear," Dr. Gray said. "We may still be able to salvage this."

"Of course," Roger said.

"Here comes Larry in the other jeep," Stan added.

Daphne heard the second jeep pull up beside the first, and more voices added to the conversation, Dave's rowdy voice among them. She couldn't make them all out, but there were at least eight. A third jeep arrived. As they gathered, they were reminded again to watch what they said.

Daphne would be unable to cross Central Valley until after they completed their search. Even there among the reeds, she would be found, and if she made a run for Prisoners Harbor, she wouldn't make it across the valley in time to avoid the search party. Now was the time to move, while the group organized itself, but she'd have to go another way. She crept low in the water, moving against the stream, back in the direction she came, hoping Cam and Phillip wouldn't head her off. Her best hope was to go around the resort along the coastline while everyone else was in Central Valley. She would have to go all the way around the island to Scorpion Anchorage.

CHAPTER SIXTEEN

Surprise on the Beach

Daphne crawled along the bottom of the stream against the current until it became shallow, and she was forced to stand. Crouching, she dashed behind a scrawny shrub, a poor cover, and then zipped up a dusty canyon ridge toward the southeast, stopping behind a boulder to catch her breath. From the safe cover of the boulder to the top of the ridge was nothing but a gravelly slope. Although she couldn't be seen from Central Valley, anyone on Sierra Blanca could easily spot her if they happened to be looking this way. But time was precious, so she took the risk and dashed up the hill and then flattened herself against the canyon ridge, prone, eyes peeking over the other side, as the ancient Indians who once inhabited the island must have done when strangers docked their boats.

On the other side of the canyon ridge, Willows Anchorage, the private pier of the resort, came into view. Empty of both people and boats, the dock was occupied by a flock of pelicans.

Daphne climbed to her feet and ran down the steep gravelly canyon wall. She slipped and fell on her hip, ripping her shorts, but got up and kept running, even though her skin stung where the rocks had rubbed her raw. If only a boat would come and take her back to the mainland. But Hortense Gray once said this was the private dock of the resort.

She ran past the pier toward the bluffs where she had watched Stan leap into the ocean a few days ago. She still couldn't believe he could betray her. It was strange, but she felt as betrayed by Stan as she had by

Cam even though she hadn't known Stan long. Cam was her best friend, but she had begun to think of Stan as the big brother she had always wished Joey could be.

The bluffs were steeper from this side than she realized coming down the canyon wall. She reached her out hands and pulled her body up the bluffs.

Scaling the bluffs reminded her of climbing the rock wall at her old gym at Alamo Heights, except here she had no gear and harness supporting her. Yet, as she dug her feet one at a time into shallow ledges, she felt surprisingly elated. Maybe it was because she had made it this far, so close to the resort without having been found.

She reached the top and flattened to her belly, remembering what Cam once said about the watchers: they could see her and Cam down on the beach even if they couldn't hear them. They might be able to see her up here as well. She crawled like a soldier across the top, her elbows and knees rubbed raw and stinging.

From here the ocean appeared less brutal, and she considered leaping in like Stan had done that morning a few days ago. He had done it repeatedly and had loved it. If he could do it, why couldn't she?

And if the water slammed her into the stone and killed her, would it matter?

She recalled the glass-bottom pool and how much pleasure she took from swimming a few days ago. While kayaking, too, before the incident with the tide, she had been fascinated and excited and full of a kind of joy. The sea lions and sting rays and the falls, the paintings on the walls, the crystal water reflecting the bright sun, all had made her happy. Being with Cam again had rejuvenated her and made her feel alive. Maybe it was possible to live and be happy as long as she didn't have to face the people she had let down. Maybe she didn't need to kill herself. She could run away and start over where no one knew her.

She scooted over the top and gazed down at the pristine beach below. The yellow poppies on the hills opposite her waved to her in the distance. As she soaked in their beauty, hoping for the strength to continue down the other side of the bluffs, a guy on the boardwalk caught her eye.

She wondered why this able-bodied person wasn't with the rest of the search party. He gazed out over the water and then descended the steps toward the beach. As he neared the coastline, her jaw dropped open and goose bumps popped out all over her arms and legs. The guy looked exactly like Brock.

It couldn't be!

He slipped off his sandals and put his feet in the water. He glanced up in her direction and she flattened as far down as she could without taking her eyes from him. The look of his face only further confirmed her suspicions. He had the same brown hair and square neck and jaw. He turned the other way, toward the poppies. She quickly scooted to the edge overlooking the ocean and scaled down the bluffs and out of his view. When she was close enough to the water, she dived past the crashing waves out as far as she could reach in the cold water and swam at a diagonal against the current as hard as she could so as not to be slammed back into the bluffs.

When she resurfaced, huffing for breath, she saw the guy running toward her. She stiffened, unable to react. She had hoped to go unnoticed. Where could she go? What should she do? Swim out to sea? She was a strong swimmer, but she was tired and starving and suddenly terrified.

"Daphne, my God. You're alive!"

It was Brock running toward her through the waves.

He wrapped his arms around her.

She melted into the familiar feel of those strong arms encircling her and for a moment forgot their history. There was only now, this moment, in his arms, and she leaned into him, exhausted and relieved. Tears ran down her face. Then reality set in as she felt the sting of her sunburn, and she pushed herself away from him.

"What are you doing here?" she asked, her eyes drawn to his thick, luscious lips.

"I wanted to go search for you with the others, but they said to wait here, in case you made it back."

"I mean here on the island. We have to get out of here."

He followed her through the waves toward the shore. "What do you mean?"

"These people are crazy. Why did you come here?"

"Because of the letter."

She stopped. "What letter?"

"The one you wrote."

"Brock, I didn't write you a letter."

"Not me, your parents."

"I didn't write them a letter."

He looked confused, his brows bent. His blue eyes, deep and endless like the sky, narrowed.

"Follow me," she said as she took his hand and led him to the poppies. There was a thin strip of beach, now that the tide was low, between the hills and the ocean where she hoped they couldn't be seen from beyond the boardwalk. Dizzy and light-headed, she sat on a rock. "Now tell me. What letter?"

She hadn't seen him in months, and he looked good—in his snug shirt and plaid shorts, skin tanned and longer hair whipping in the wind all around his bright blue eyes. When he touched her, it burned, but not because she was sunburnt. He burned a charge through her, like jump-starting a dead battery.

He sat opposite her. "They got a letter from you saying you were on this island and someone stole your credit card, and you couldn't leave the hotel without paying fifty thousand dollars in charges, or they'd arrest you, could they send money."

"I never wrote that."

"What? Then who…"

"They're stealing money. That's what this is really about." She couldn't believe it, but she should have known, because everything was always about money.

It occurred to her that Brock could be in on it and the whole bit about the letter and the credit card charges was a lie. What if what Cam had said about her mother sending her here for therapy was true and Brock had been brought in to help?

"Your mom was worried. She asked me to come."

"Did you just arrive?"

"Wasn't easy to find this place. Kept getting the run-around."

"So you got here today?"

"Yeah, this morning. Couldn't believe it when they didn't know where you were."

"What did they say? Who'd you talk to?"

"This black chick named Hortense Gray. Said you went off exploring and hadn't returned. She took your mom's check but wouldn't let me help with the search. In fact, she didn't seem pleased to see me. Wants me on the first boat out of here."

"They play strange games here. I was almost killed when a horse threw me."

"Are you joking?"

She searched his eyes. "Tell me the truth about what you know. I'm really tired."

"All I know is what your mother told me. You were almost killed?"

"Yes. And then I had a gun trained on me."

"A gun? Jesus!"

"We got to get off this island. We'll have to follow the coastline all the way back to Scorpion Anchorage."

"That's toward the mainland, right? We passed that coming in."

"Yeah. Let's get going." Daphne turned to go, but Brock grabbed her arm and turned her to face him. Again, a charge jolted through her from his skin through hers, something more than the sting of her burned skin.

"Wait. When was the last time you ate or drank anything?"

She pulled her arm away. "They're searching for me as we speak. Come on."

"The resort is dead except for a few women lounging by the pool. This one chick named Emma started flirting with me till she got my name. She said, 'Daphne's Brock?' I hadn't heard that in a while." He gave her a warm smile.

Daphne blushed and lowered her eyes, and the pain of what she had done flooded over her. If only she had gotten out of bed. "Yeah, well…"

"Let me run back and get some food and water and my wallet, so I can get us back home, if you're sure that's what we should do."

"If I'm sure? What did I just tell you? They had a gun on me!"

"And you know they're connected with the resort?"

"Brock, trust me."

"You gotta know how freaky it all sounds."

"I know."

"Let me get some stuff. I'll be right back."

Daphne crossed her arms and thought about this. She might be a sitting duck waiting here for Brock. "I'll go on ahead another mile or so and wait for you. Don't stop to talk to anyone if you can avoid it."

He started to touch her shoulder but stopped. "You're so burnt."

"Listen Brock, there are cameras everywhere. They even had a camera on a fox trained to follow me." The memory of his little body curled helplessly in her arms made her wince. "I'm telling you this place is crazy, so be careful."

He stared at her and didn't say anything.

"Are you listening?"

"Yeah. I'll catch up with you."

He touched her hair, then bent and kissed the top of her head. Heat surged through her all the way down to her toes.

"I've missed you, Daph." He turned to go. "I'll find you. Keep an eye out for me."

It took her several minutes to recover. She hadn't seen Brock since New Year's Day when he came to see her in the hospital. She hadn't wanted visitors because she was still getting used to the idea that she was alive, but he had come anyway. She wouldn't look at him, wouldn't talk to him. He had said he would pray for her and had left.

Before that, it had been November. She had just dropped out of her senior year of high school even though Brock had begged her not to do it.

"You're so close," he had said.

But Kara didn't get to graduate. Joey didn't get to graduate. Why should she when it was all her fault that they hadn't? She could have saved Kara's life had she gotten out of bed. And saving Kara might have stopped Joey from falling off the deep end.

Two weeks after she dropped out, Brock came to say they should take a break. She didn't see him again until New Year's Day—the day that wasn't supposed to come for her.

And today, six months later, he took her in his arms like they were good friends, maybe even boyfriend and girlfriend, like nothing had gone wrong. Had her mother made him feel obligated to come, or had he wanted to see her?

Tears rushed from her eyes as she hiked along the thin strip of beach near the poppies toward the east, weak and dizzy and her hip hurting from where she had fallen and scraped it. A yellowish bruise formed around it.

Why had Brock come?

She laughed at herself, out loud, scaring a gull from its perch on a nearby rock. Here she was being tormented by a bunch of freaks on a remote island and her primary thought was about Brock's motives?

Come on, Daphne.

But she couldn't help herself. She had made him miserable with her inability to ever be happy again. She wouldn't allow herself to be happy and she didn't want Brock to suffer, so she had begun to shut him out little by little until he couldn't take it anymore and left her. In another world where Kara was still alive, where Joey hadn't electrocuted Grandpa and then sunk into psychosis, in that world, Daphne would love Brock like she could love no other and they would live happily ever after.

But this wasn't that world. So why had he come? He could have told her mother no, if she had indeed asked him to come—whether to bring the check as he had said or to participate in the therapeutic games. Either way, he could have said no, and he hadn't.

CHAPTER SEVENTEEN

The Body Beneath the Pier

The thin strip of beach ended with more massive rocks for Daphne to climb if she was to make her way around the coastline to Scorpion Anchorage. As she reached up with her hands to find a grip, she saw her own burnt arms, and the stinging she'd been only mildly aware of hit her full force. She gritted her teeth and bore the pain, for there was nothing else to do, and she climbed the rock, little by little, searching for lodgments for her feet, finding a new grip, heaving herself up, until she was, at last, on top, only to find another rock must be climbed to move forward. The sun baked her, but the wind had picked up, cooling her the higher she climbed. When she reached the summit, she looked to the east where the island curved north, and though she could not see Scorpion Anchorage, she was amazed to see the coast of California and hundreds of boats in the distance. None of them were close enough to see her, but the sight of them filled her with tremendous hope, and she leapt in the air, waving her arms. She would get off this island. She could feel it.

Realizing she might make herself more visible to those following her, she stopped gallivanting about and jogged across the headland, passing an old wooden sign that read "Bowen Point," and scaled down the side of the bluff to where the rocky terrain sloped inland through a thin copse of scraggily trees. Further inland, the brush grew thicker and the trees taller, but here the leaves were few and the shade hardly worth standing in. Because her skin stung, she stood there for a moment, the approaching bank barely visible between the jutting rocks. She could stay there and wait for Brock, but the landscape penned her in and provided little chance of escaping if the wrong person were to discover her, so she trudged onward toward the bank, between the rocky cliff-edges on either side, and out onto a sandy embankment leading, in the distance, to another pier.

Although this strip of sand was wider than the one by the poppies, it was encroached upon my massive slabs of rock divided by gaps, one of which had led her from the scraggily trees to where she now stood. But there were other gaps between the crags, and the notion that someone might appear through one of them at any moment urged her past them toward the pier.

The sand was as pristine here as the beach at the resort, and although she jogged across it, she couldn't help but appreciate the way the water, with its diamond-like sparkle from the sunshine, lapped up to meet it. She could still see the boats miles off in the distance and on the horizon toward the east, not as visible from Bowen Point, the mainland.

As she approached the pier, she noticed a sea cave tucked beneath the last mound of rock where the beach gave way to ocean, so she passed the pier and jogged down to the last foot of sand and peered inside. The water was deep where it rushed into the cave, and she imagined there might be all manner of sea life thriving there. Sure enough, before she took her eyes away to inspect the ceiling, she saw a stingray circle at the surface and disappear again into the depths of the water. She recalled what Larry had said about the stingrays and the tide and realized it must be coming in. Before seeking higher ground, she looked up at the walls of the cave as far back as she could and was amazed by the presence of petroglyphs, like those in the caves Larry had taken her to in the kayaks. Dolphins, sea lions, sharks, pelicans, and other figures were visible in crude form carved and painted along with other symbols Daphne did not recognize.

A rush of water covered her shoes, reminding her of the tide, so she turned back up the embankment toward the high rocks, when an object floating beneath the pier caught her eye.

A hump of pale gray, resembling a dead dolphin, rocked back and forth with the waves. She walked to the edge of the sand to the wooden steps to get a better look. Still unable to make it out, she climbed the steps and peered over the edge. It was hung up on one of the wooden legs of the dock, rocking, but not drifting, with the tide.

She stopped and stared, and the more she stared, the more it resembled a person floating on his back. A dead person.

A cry of shock fled from her throat, and she covered her mouth, trying not to be sick. Just then, a wave loosened the body from the pier, and it rolled in the water three-hundred-sixty degrees, returning to its back. That's when she saw the face and realized who it was.

"Pete!" Maybe he wasn't dead. "Pete!"

The body didn't move except with the tide toward the island.

"Pete, can you hear me?"

The water rolled him over again, and now he was face down, rushing along the shore toward the sea cave. Another wave took him under, and she lost sight of him for a long moment until he popped up again, several feet away at the mouth of the cave. He rolled once more, landing on his back, but his face remained without expression.

"Pete!"

She thought of jumping in and shaking him. Maybe he was simply knocked unconscious and was still alive, but before she could act on this idea another wave swept him into the cave. Daphne climbed down the wooden steps and ran back down the bank to where the water reached her knees, following Pete until his body disappeared in the dark depths of the cavern.

Should she follow?

The water slapped against her chest, threatening to wash her in after him, but too frightened by what sea life might be lurking there, and even more frightened of getting trapped underwater by the tide, she ran against the current back to high ground and through a gap in the crags to the grassy knolls further inland.

Poor Pete!

Once she caught her breath, she climbed over the sea cave and further east, away from the high rocks to a gentler terrain of sand and dirt and grass, and, wonder of wonders, a giant sprawling oak with real shade. She went to it.

Oh my God, Pete! And again, out loud, inexplicably, she cried, "Kara!"

She rubbed her eyes as sweat and tears blinded her, and nausea threatened to make her vomit. Pete must have failed in the kayak. He'd been so desperate to get off the island, he'd sacrificed his life! She fell beneath the oak and wept.

Poor Pete. Now his son would never have the opportunity to invite him to visit in Costa Rica, and his brand-new granddaughter would never meet him, nor would his daughter, Daphne's age, ever set eyes on her father again. Tears slid down her face, and the image of Pete floating and rolling in the sea made her stomach churn. If she had believed before that Stan and his gun might have been one more exercise in a strange therapy, she could no longer. With Pete dead, there was no doubt in her mind she and Brock were in danger and needed to find a way off the island as soon as possible.

For now, she would wait here for Brock since it was open to multiple escape routes and had low branches to hide her as she sat on the ground facing the sea with her back to the thick trunk. Brock would pass by here, if he came this far—suddenly she worried she had gone too far. Too exhausted and upset to turn back, she sat there, determined to give him a chance to catch up with her and hoping he'd come.

She couldn't believe Cam had brought her here. She suddenly worried he, too, might be in danger. Maybe he didn't know what was really going on. That was the only reasonable explanation. But she couldn't save him without getting caught. He'd be better off if she got off the island and returned with help. She'd get the police or the FBI.

As the sun sank behind the rocks, Daphne sat beneath the sprawling, thick oak, which was probably as old as the island, wishing she had gone back for Brock. She shivered in the breeze, her red skin breaking out into goose flesh, her body sore and tired.

Why hadn't he found her yet?

<u>CHAPTER EIGHTEEN</u>

A Dark Night

Not for the first time, Daphne worried Brock had been detained by someone at the resort. Maybe they had him at gunpoint, just as they'd had her, hoping she'd come for him and right into their trap. If she weren't so exhausted and dizzy and sore, she would have gone back by now instead of sitting beneath the giant oak with her eyes closed.

For the past few hours her mantra had been, "A few more minutes."

"When the sun sits beneath the cloud bank, I'll go," she had said. But when the sun was no longer shrouded in white, she cringed, exhausted and weak. "When it reaches that headland, I'll go." Once again, she could not muster up the strength.

Now the sun was no longer visible from where it set on the other side of the island, and soon dusk would settle over her, and then darkness. Although she was frightened of spending the night in the dark alone, she knew there were worse things, and so had resigned to stay.

She might have been happy to sit there with the old oak tree, confident the search for her would be put off for the night, if it weren't for her fear that they'd harmed Brock. Sure, they would use him for bait, but that didn't mean he'd be *live* bait.

Then it occurred to her he might have injured himself on his way to find her and could be lying on the beach or at the bottom of a ravine unable to go on. The memory of Pete being swept by the tide into the cave chilled her. Brock could be dying, and here she was on her butt against a tree. She had to go back and look for him. She couldn't make the same mistake she'd made with Kara.

She climbed to her feet, using the tree for balance, her legs wobbly and her back sore. Finding her footing in the sandy dirt, she trudged swiftly in the direction she came, aware that dusk was upon her and night was coming. She climbed up the hill toward the rocky crags above the sea cave that had swallowed Pete and then down past the pier along the beach as dusk gave in to darkness. The steep bluffs of Bowen's Point made her cry as she dragged herself back up to the summit. She had zero energy and was on the verge of fainting from lack of food and water. But she made it up to the headland and the old wooden sign. She fell to her knees to catch her breath.

When she lifted her head toward the mainland, she was shocked by all the beautiful lights shining from the California coastline. She could imagine all the people safely in the cities dining in restaurants, watching movies at the cinema, listening to iPhones, playing online computer games, drinking coffee, and driving back and forth along the highway to visit friends and relatives. At one time, she had been among them but hadn't realized how lucky she was. She had eaten in restaurants and had gone to movies and such, but she hadn't appreciated her freedom and safety because of the guilt and shame she carried around. She had been miserable, even in the safety of her own home, feeling she couldn't allow herself to enjoy life when she had ruined it for so many others. But now, standing on the summit of Bowen Point gazing across the dark oblivion that was the ocean, she knew, as she longed to be back on the mainland, that, if given the chance, she'd change. She thought so, anyway, standing there at that moment. Maybe she wouldn't. Maybe it would be too hard. Maybe she'd go back to the way things were. But she wanted to believe she could allow herself to be happy, to forgive herself and to realize Kara, her parents, and even Joey would prefer her to be happy.

She heard the sound of rocks sliding to her right where a beam of light danced at the top of the headland. Her heart fluttered as she grabbed the nearest rock for a weapon and cautiously peered down. Brock clambered up with a light attached to a cap on his head. She dropped the rock with relief.

"Where have you been?" She took his arm and helped him to the top. "I've been so worried."

He hunched over, breathing heavily, and, when he could, said, "Man, Daph, when you said you were going ahead, I didn't know you meant this far. Hell, you've crossed half the island." He shrugged out of his backpack and dropped it at her feet.

She threw her arms around him and burst into tears. "Oh, Brock!"

He held her close and kissed the top of her head. "It's okay. It's okay. I'm sorry it took so long."

"I saw a dead body. Someone I met earlier today." She shuddered. "His name was Pete."

"What are you talking about?"

"Over down there by the pier. The current swept him under a cave. I couldn't get to him."

"Are you sure he was dead?"

"If he wasn't then, he is now. What are we going to do?"

Brock stepped back and dropped to his bottom on the rock. "I can't believe it."

"I told you, this place is dangerous." She sat close beside him, unzipping the pack for water. She drank down an entire bottle in a less than a minute.

"It must have been another trick."

"Brock, I saw him with my own eyes."

"He must have been acting."

"Why do you keep saying that?"

"Dr. Gray told me all about this place, about the therapy, about your parents sending you here. That's what took me so long to come find you. I'm not supposed to let on I know. I'm supposed to get you back to the resort in the morning—it's too dark and dangerous to attempt it tonight."

"What?" Daphne was incredulous and began to tremble with anger and confusion. "I told you, they had a gun. Stan had a gun pointed right at me."

"It wasn't loaded. It was all an act."

"But Pete—"

"He was in on it. That's why I can't believe he's dead."

"Hortense Gray said he was in on it? She said *Pete* was in on it? But Pete ran away, like me. He was going to get help."

"She explained everything to me. Cam was there, too."

"You saw Cam?" She could feel the heat rush to her sunburnt face. "He was with them?"

"And Stan and Larry. A whole group of them. Dr. Gray had me follow her into the main building and they told me all about what they do for the people who come here. I wasn't supposed to tell you yet, but I can see how upset you are and, like I told them, I'm no actor. They shouldn't have asked me to lie to you."

A blast of wind blew against them and whipped her ponytail into her face. The sky was dark, the stars not visible above the gray clouds, which were also barely discernible in the soft, distilled light of the half moon. Daphne shivered, dumbstruck, trying to process all that Brock had said.

"But the horse threw me. I could have been killed."

"They said that was an accident, and they're upset about it. They're worried they'll be shut down."

"They should be."

"They said they herded you back to this part of the island. They knew you'd run, and if you hadn't, another actor would have found you and brought you here. They have that Gregory guy on standby. I think he likes you."

"Gregory Gray?" Her mouth dropped open for the umpteenth time.

Brock shrugged.

"I don't believe it. They're lying. Larry told me this place was about the watchers, not therapy for me. Larry said that. You can't believe anything they tell you."

The two of them sat in the darkness and the quiet and said nothing more for many minutes. Daphne opened another water bottle and ate more of the food—crackers and slices of cheese and summer sausage. The grapes were like explosions of wonderful as she popped them into her mouth and bit down.

"Look, I know you're tired," Brock finally said. "Dr. Gray sent a sleeping bag, knowing we'd be caught out here." He tugged it loose from the pack and unrolled it.

"Only one?"

He cracked a smile. "Two would've been too bulky to carry."

"I see."

"She also sent sunscreen and ointment for sunburns. Let me put some of this on your back and shoulders."

Although the ointment gave her goose bumps, it soothed her burnt skin and brought her relief. Sounds of pleasure escaped from her lips as he coated the cream across her back where her halter top had failed to protect her.

"This bruise doesn't look too good," he said.

"That's where I fell off the horse."

"Am I hurting you?"

"A little, but it mostly feels wonderful."

He rubbed more of it along her shoulders and arms. She reached for the tube so she could apply some to her legs and face, but he snatched it away and whispered, "Let me."

So, she closed her eyes as he gently applied the cream all over her sore, tired, burning body. Over and over, she said, "Oh, thank you. Thank you."

When he had finished, he unzipped the sleeping bag and crawled inside. "I'm sorry all this has happened to you, and I honestly don't know what to think. I doubt your parents would've sent you here if they knew what it was really like."

"Did my mother actually tell you she and Dad sent me here?"

"No. She told me about a letter and asked me to bring a check. Dr. Gray said that was all to get me to the island."

"You weren't expecting…"

"No."

"They could be lying. Don't you see? Wouldn't my parents have said something to you?"

"I don't know. I don't know what to think."

"Bet you're sorry you got mixed up in all of this."

He lay down and linked his hands behind his head, gazing up at the sky. "I'm not sorry, Daph. I've missed you."

Her throat tightened, and tears rushed to her eyes. "Really?"

"Yeah. I've been hoping you'd call."

"*You* could have called."

"Wouldn't do any good if you weren't ready."

She thought about that. "No. I guess not."

"I've been in touch with your parents."

"Checking up on me?"

"Of course. But they never seemed to know anything either. We're all so worried about you. Especially after last New Year's."

"Don't talk about that."

They were quiet again, until he said, "Come here."

She screwed the lid back onto the plastic water bottle and climbed into the sleeping bag beside Brock, resting her head on the crook of his arm. As she stretched her body and relaxed, an involuntary sigh escaped her lips.

"It's too bad we can't see the stars," Brock said.

Daphne closed her eyes. "I'm too tired to care."

"Try to get some sleep. I won't let anything else happen to you. If you want to leave the island, I'll make it happen."

She couldn't resist giving him a soft kiss on his cheek. "I'm so glad you're here. I'm not as scared now."

He leaned over and touched his lips to hers. Tears slid from the corners of her eyes and dripped down to her ears.

"God, Daph, it's been so hard without you."

She yielded to his kisses and kissed him back, wrapping her arms around his waist and turning to her side to press her sore body against his. "I'm so sorry," she whispered in between kisses. "I'm so sorry I hurt you."

His warm, damp tears bled onto her cheeks, and she pressed her hand against his back and pulled herself hard against him.

"I still love you, you know," he said.

"I know. I know. Oh, Brock." She kissed him again. "I love you, too. It was never about that."

"I know." He rubbed her sunburnt arm.

"Ow."

"Sorry. I can feel the heat coming off your skin. Poor Daph. Try to get some rest now."

She nestled against him and closed her eyes and felt at peace.

CHAPTER NINETEEN

Love Beneath the Oak

Sometime in the middle of the night, the clouds broke. Brock whipped the sleeping bag over their heads, but soon they were drenched, Daphne's newly burnt skin unable to keep her warm in the wind. She shivered all over.

They struggled from the bag and gathered their things with the light on Brock's cap providing little help in the thick rain. The lightning in the distance illuminated the headland as they made their way down toward the east. The rain turned the white stone slick beneath their feet, and, as they scaled down the side, they slipped and half-fell to the next level of rock before finding the path to the beach. They ran across the now-wet sand, past the pier, and through the narrow gaps between the crags, resting for a moment beneath a cliff edge, but because it provided no protection, they ran on until they came upon the sprawling old oak.

They crawled beneath the thick branches and sat with their backs against the trunk, shivering and panting beside one another. Only some of the deluge made its way down to them through the manifold of twisted branches and leaves all around them.

"Are you okay?" Brock put an arm around Daphne.

She nodded. "Just cold."

"The sleeping bag's worthless."

Shivering, teeth chattering, unable to speak, she nestled against his wet, warm body. He lifted her chin and pressed his wet lips against hers, sending shocks of heat through her.

He whispered at her ear, "I'll take care of you. Go back to sleep."

Wrapped in his arms, his warm breath against her neck, she relaxed and, despite the torrent, fell asleep.

In the morning, Daphne was awakened by the sound of her own name being whispered near her ear.

She smiled and opened her eyes and stretched under the oak tree with the damp sleeping bag beneath her head and her own hair tickling the sides of her face with the gentle breeze. The water lapped the shore a dozen yards away, and the sun, low in the cloudless sky, hid behind the rocky bluffs. A hundred birds called out to one another from where they roosted in the thick branches above.

Where was Brock? She sat up and looked around, her stomach clenching.

This is not the haunted side of the island.

The whisper came again, this time behind her. "Daphne."

She jumped to her feet and ran in all directions but saw no one. Could it have been the swaying of the leaves?

Out in the sea, Brock jumped over the waves with his hands in the air, his bare back to her, and he was shouting, "Woo, hoo!" repeatedly.

A smile crossed her face at the sight of his revelry, and she decided she was just tired and edgy and was hearing things that weren't real. She fished through the backpack for more grapes and then, carrying a bunch, walked across the sand to join Brock in the sea.

The cold water crawled up her legs toward her thighs, and she let out a squeal when it reached her waist.

"Hey," Brock said. "You look happier this morning."

"Should we head to Scorpion Anchorage right away?"

"They think I'm bringing you back, remember? They won't search for us for a while."

She popped a grape into her mouth. "Want one?"

"No thanks. Sleep alright?"

"Guess so. You?"

"Best night of sleep I've had in months."

Daphne laughed. "You had your best sleep against an old oak tree during a storm, soaked, cold, and without a proper bed?"

"Yep." He stole a grape from the bunch and popped it into his mouth with a wink.

Even though she teased him, she felt the same way. She had felt at peace in his arms.

"Brock," Daphne's mouth went dry. "What if I can't do this? What if it's like last time?" She hadn't meant to ask him that. The words spilled out.

His smile dropped at the corners, and he gazed at the sea. Then he turned his blue eyes to her and said, "Don't worry about hurting me. I won't be any worse off the second time." He moved closer and put his arms around her. "If you're willing, it's worth it to me to try again."

She buried her face in his bare chest, warm and wet and hard with muscle. She wanted to kiss him and to leave him at the same time. "I'm scared."

"Don't be. Try to enjoy life as much as you can. Let go of the past."

She pulled away and took several steps back. "But that's the problem. I can't. I don't know how."

"If it had been you and not Kara, if Kara had heard but hadn't gotten up, would you want Kara to be miserable for the rest of her life?"

"Of course not."

"What if she's watching you from heaven? What if she has to witness your suffering?"

"Are you going to say I'm selfish again?"

"I shouldn't have said that. I'm sorry." He stepped toward her.

She narrowed her eyes, unable to control how defensive and angry she felt. "But you believe it, don't you?"

"No. I understand better now. I've done a lot of research on survivor's guilt, which is what you have."

"No shit, Sherlock." She gasped at her own cruelty. "I'm sorry. Oh, Brock. I didn't mean that."

He clenched his jaw and walked past her toward the shore. "It's okay."

She followed him. "What did you discover, in your research? Anything helpful?"

"Sure."

"Like what?"

"Like it's easier to believe you could have done something to change what happened than to accept your own helplessness."

She stopped dead in her tracks, the water washing over her calves.

He stopped, too, and looked back at her.

She thought about that. Was that what she was doing? No.

"I *could* have done something. If I'd gotten out of bed, Kara would be alive."

"Maybe." He kept walking. "Maybe not. Maybe you'd be dead, too. We'll never know."

She followed him through the waves toward the beach and back to the oak. She thought about what he'd said. Was she fooling herself into thinking she could have prevented Kara's death?

She wished it had been her instead of Kara. Tears sprang to her eyes as she peeled through the branches and sat against the thick trunk of the tree. Brock dusted off and rolled up the sleeping bag.

"It should have been me," she said out loud. "I don't mean to sound like a baby, but it's true. She was smarter, and faster, and prettier, and I was so jealous of her. I hate that about myself. I wish I could have been happy for her, but I wanted to be better than her, and I wasn't—not at one single thing." The tears ran down her cheeks and her body shuddered. "I hate my self-pity, but I really do believe even my parents wish it had been me instead of Kara."

Brock knelt on the ground and tied up the sleeping bag to the backpack, shaking his head. "No wonder you're miserable."

Daphne's mouth fell open. "Wouldn't you be?"

He stood up with his hands on his slim hips and looked down at her. "First of all, I doubt they wish it had been you. *You* wish it had been you. They wish it had been *them*. That's survivor's guilt. But let's say your parents are cruel enough to wish it had been you instead of Kara. Then they're assholes and you have to cut them loose and go on with your life, because your life has value."

"They aren't assholes."

"Any parent who wishes one child was dead in place of another is an asshole, Daphne, plain and simple."

"They can't help it. Kara was so good."

"And you're not?"

"I'm not *as* good."

He crossed his arms in front of his chest and frowned. "Why do you say that?"

How had they gotten into this? Daphne wanted to stand up and run away, to the other side of the island—anything but talk about this. *Because*, that's why! She wanted to scream, *Because!* Before she knew what she was saying, she was shouting, "Do you know what the last thing I said to her was? She had borrowed my favorite Hollister shirt without asking. I didn't know until we got home from school—she was in junior high and I was a sophomore—and I made her take it off right away, right there in the living room, afraid she'd get her supper stains all over it. When she took it off and handed it to me, I," she broke into sobs and shouted through the lump in her throat, "I swung it at her and told her she should ask next time. She said she would have asked, but she left for school earlier that morning and didn't want to wake me up, and Mama said it was okay. I yelled that it was my shirt, not Mama's, and I was planning on wearing it. She said all her shirts were getting too small.

"I was such a bitch. Who cares about a shirt? I was fifteen and she thirteen and I was hitting her with a stupid Hollister shirt. The truth is she looked better in it. We didn't speak to each other all night. Joey had heard us screaming at each other, and he sided with me. He wouldn't have thought she was possessed if I hadn't gotten so mad at her…wouldn't have gone to her room. Oh, Brock! Don't you see? My stupid tantrum, my idiotic jealousy, made him kill her!" Daphne covered her face with her hands, so ashamed. She hadn't told anyone this and hadn't meant to. She didn't want anyone to know how petty she had been, how mean she had been to her sweet sister the day before she died, and how truly, unalterably, Kara's death had been her fault.

Brock fell to his knees and took Daphne in his arms. He held her so tight that it hurt, but it hurt in a good way, a comforting way, and she was glad. He didn't say anything but held her until she stopped shaking and sobbing and was still.

At last he kissed her forehead and said, "Maybe one day you'll see how typical that was, fighting with your sister over a borrowed shirt, and how impossible it was to know it would set Joey off, if it even did. Now let me put some of this sunscreen on you."

"Wait a minute." She searched his eyes. "Are you still saying it wasn't my fault, even after what I just said to you?"

"That's what I'm saying." He took his shirt from the backpack. "Here, you wear my shirt and help me with this sunscreen."

She sat beneath the oak lathering the sunscreen across his back and her own arms and legs in stunned silence. Brock still didn't think it was her fault, even after hearing the whole story. She'd told no one, sure everyone would despise her even more than they already did. Why didn't Brock despise her?

When they finished applying the sunscreen, Brock got up and helped her to her feet, swung the backpack across his shoulders, took her hand, and led her east, toward Scorpion Anchorage.

CHAPTER TWENTY

Trouble in the Woods

Daphne marched beside Brock across the sandy beach, mulling over his reaction to her confession. She was shocked outright that he hadn't condemned her. Maybe love had blinded him. The alternative seemed so unlikely: that perhaps she *wasn't* responsible for Kara's death.

She took another sip from her water bottle, resisting the urge to drink it all down at once. There was only one other left in the backpack, and she had no idea how much longer it would take them to reach Scorpion Anchorage.

They followed the coastline as the hot sun blazed down on them. For the first half hour they talked about what they had each been doing over the past six months. Brock had been attending Trinity University in San Antonio with a swimming scholarship and was majoring in kinesiology. He talked about some of his classes and meets without mentioning the dream they once shared: they were going to open their own swim school together one day. She told him she'd been in a funk and hadn't done much of anything. She didn't add that she'd spent her time finding ways to end her life. That now seemed like such a long time ago.

I can be happy, as long as I'm away from my family.

She pushed away thoughts of Kara and Joey and tried not to imagine her mother's wide eyes the morning they found Kara.

Daphne took a deep breath and let it out slowly and sipped more water. She noticed Brock's water bottle was already empty.

"Do you ever think about going back to school?" Brock asked. "You were so close to graduating."

That had been the last thing on Daphne's mind, but now she thought maybe she would go back, not to their old high school, but someplace else where people didn't know her.

"Maybe. I think about moving away and starting over."

He squeezed her hand. "Do you see me in the picture?"

She smiled. "Hmm." Any picture would look nicer with him in it, but out loud she said, "I'm still thinking about it."

He returned her smile, though he looked hurt, and she wished she could take it back. As they walked along the surf, trying to stay cool with their shoes in the water, she kept her eyes out toward the sea in search of boats. The only ones visible were too far away. Occasionally, she'd wave her arms at one that seemed closer than the others, but this had no effect.

"So where would you go?' he asked after a while.

"Huh?"

"You said you think about moving away and starting over. Where?"

"Anywhere. It doesn't matter."

"If you had a choice, and could choose anywhere, where would it be?"

"Hmm. It used to be someplace with a beach, but not anymore." She laughed. "Maybe Alaska?"

"That would be a pretty big change from Texas."

"Yeah. And I don't really like the cold." She picked up a shell and threw it into the ocean. "I don't know. Maybe Europe. Maybe Paris or London."

"I'd want to go to Colorado and live in the mountains."

"I guess our swim school would have to be indoors." She couldn't believe she said that.

He gave her a look of surprise and then smiled. "Yeah. It would have to be."

After an hour or so, she let go of Brock's hand and bent over the surf to wet her arms and legs. It was just too dang hot.

When they trudged across the sand around a bluff, Daphne couldn't believe her eyes. Trees! These weren't the scraggily trees she'd seen so far on the island, with the exception of the huge, ancient oak; these were tall, lush, and *multiple* trees. In fact, collectively, they could even be called a *forest*.

"Let's get you out of this sun," Brock said, also noticing them. "Before you turn into a lobster."

The canopy was thick and blocked most of the sunlight. Consequently the ground consisted of dirt and rock and very little grass or undergrowth. It took a few minutes for Daphne's eyes to adjust from the blinding sun on the beach to the near-darkness in the woods. She stopped for a moment, closed her eyes, and sighed. The drop in temperature was immediate.

"Oh, it's so much better here," she said as her entire body relaxed. "It's even pleasant."

"Let's find a place to rest and eat."

Brock continued through the woods, so Daphne followed, until they came upon a flat area, relatively free of rocks, next to a thick trunk, where the two of them could sit side by side on the smooth, packed dirt. They took out the leftover crackers, slices of cheese, and summer sausage, and Daphne shared her remaining water bottle with Brock, both of them agreeing to save the last bottle for as long as they could stand it. They also ate some of the grapes but would reserve the majority of them as well. Although Daphne could have eaten three times as much as they had, the snack would do. Surely they'd manage to find their way off the island before the end of the day.

"Oh, I'm so tired, and this feels so nice," Daphne said.

"Let's sit here for a bit, then."

"I guess a little break wouldn't hurt."

"I'm pretty sure boats come and go all day long at Scorpion Anchorage."

"Man, it's all catching up with me. Every muscle in my body feels sore."

Brock put his arm across her shoulders. "Does that hurt?"

"It's okay." She leaned her head against his bare chest and closed her eyes.

"I wish we could stay like this forever," Brock said after a while.

"But not here, on this creepy island."

"The island's not creepy, it's the people. The island is beautiful."

"That's true."

"I guess I'm afraid once we get home, that…" his voice trailed off.

Daphne lifted her head and searched his face. "That what?"

"That you'll go back to ignoring me again."

She buried her face in his chest as a lump rose to her throat. "Why do you even love me?"

"How can you ask me that?"

"I'm so…broken. I'm no good."

"But that's part of it."

She lifted her head again. "What?"

"You think it's never crossed my mind to do exactly what you did last New Year's?"

"You…"

"When my mother died, I had no one. You'd think my dad would step up, but he didn't."

"I thought he called you."

"He called me one time to check on me, and that was it."

She hadn't thought about how lonely he would have been without her, or how lonely he must have become when they broke up. "We helped each other, didn't we," she said without inflection.

"We understood each other. We were *both* broken."

Had he understood her? Maybe better than she had realized. "I suppose you're right."

"Until you checked out."

That was true, she thought. "But it felt wrong."

He stopped breathing and stiffened beneath her. "Oh. I thought…"

"No. I don't mean it felt wrong being with you. I mean it felt wrong to allow myself to be happy."

"If it hadn't been for you…." He fought tears welling up in his eyes, and she wanted to throw her arms around him, but she resisted. He cleared his throat and clenched his jaw, and when he could, he said, "You saved my life, Daph. Have you ever thought of that? You're so busy blaming yourself for Kara's death. It never once occurred to you that you saved me."

Her mouth dropped open. She didn't know what to say.

The tears escaped his eyes and fell down his cheeks, and before she could wipe them away, he fiercely pressed his mouth to hers.

She felt her own tears slide down her cheeks and mix with his at their mouths, leaving a salty taste on his lips. She grabbed fistfuls of his hair and straddled his lap. She loved him. She wanted to be with him. Forever.

Then a cold shiver crawled down her spine when she heard her name whispered behind her. "Daphne."

She and Brock stopped kissing and looked around.

"Did you hear that?" Daphne asked.

Brock moved her aside and jumped to his feet. "Yes." He took her hand and pulled her up.

They looked around, holding tightly to one another, but saw no one.

Then the whisper came again. "Daphne."

"Let's get out of here." Brock grabbed the backpack and the two of them ran.

Daphne snatched glances behind her, in the direction they had heard the whisper, and saw a dark figure, maybe a man, dart behind a tree.

"Keep running," she said. "There's someone back there."

She could no longer tell which direction was east because the sun was almost completely blocked, and the woods seemed endless. It was possible they were running the wrong way or that they were running in circles. Daphne glanced back again but saw no one. Then, Brock stopped, and Daphne saw someone up ahead. It was one of the ghost girls.

Daphne grabbed Brock's hand and led him to their right, unable to believe the games reached this far.

I don't believe in ghosts.

After a few more yards, Brock stopped again. Two more ghost girls walked toward them with their arms outstretched.

"Leave us alone!" Daphne screamed.

Brock grabbed her hand and led them in the opposite direction. The man from before was bearing on them at their left.

"Faster!" Daphne said.

"We're being herded!" Brock said. "It's a trap!"

He grabbed her arm and ran toward the first ghost girl.

"What are you doing?" Daphne asked. "There might be more of them. She might have a gun."

"Stay close."

Daphne's heart slammed against her ribcage as they ran by the ghost girl, who shrieked at her as they passed, "You're one of the dead, Daphne Janus!"

Up ahead, the canopy thinned, and huge rocks jutted from the ground. Brock led her into one of many caves that cut through the rock, but she pulled back on his hand.

"No. Don't go in there. We'll be trapped."

"Shh. There are at least ten other crevices like this one. They'll pass by."

"How do you know?" she whispered.

"I'm too exhausted to keep running," he whispered back. "Come on."

"But…"

He pulled her by the hand and led her into one of the caves. It was narrow, maybe three feet wide, but tall enough for them to stand. The rocky ground was uneven. A dim light shone in from a crack above and from another opening about ten feet away.

"Oh my God," she whispered, panting and afraid. "I can't do this. You know I'm claustrophobic."

"Shh. Just close your eyes and let me hold you. Forget the cave."

Brock put both arms around her, but she couldn't breathe.

Her heart thudded in her ears. She opened her mouth, trying to catch her breath. "They could easily trap us in here."

"Be quiet, will you?"

He found a ledge and pulled her into his lap. "Shh," he warned before she could say another word.

They could hear rustling outside, the sound of shoes moving over rocks. Daphne froze, moving only her eyes from side to side, to the two openings on each end of the cave.

"They went this way!" a girl shouted.

They heard her run past the cave.

Then a face peered in through the side which Daphne and Brock had entered.

"Daphne?" It was Stan! "Are you in here?"

Daphne glanced back at Brock, who held his finger to his lips.

They remained like that, waiting and listening. Daphne didn't breathe.

After a few minutes, the rustling moved past the cave, and another shout further away indicated the group had moved on. Daphne scrambled from Brock's lap, but he grabbed her hand before she could exit the cave.

Softly he whispered. "Wait. Make sure it's not a trick."

She went into his open arms and laid her cheek against his chest, eyes closed, trying to forget the feeling of the cave walls closing in on her. He was right to wait. One of the group might have stayed behind to catch them coming out.

Brock kissed her hair and then took her face in his hands. She could barely see him in the dark. He pressed his lips to hers and then swept his mouth across her chin to her ear, and then down her throat. She sighed with pleasure and ran her hands through his hair. If he was trying to distract her, it was working. He pulled her body hard against his so that every part of her pressed against every part of him. She ran her hands along the muscles in his back, his shoulders, his arms.

His hands moved from her waist to her back, and she gasped with pain.

"My sunburn," she whispered.

"Sorry."

"It's okay. We should probably get out of here anyway."

He took the lead, heading the same way they had entered. She waited while he looked around, and then, when he beckoned her, she followed him into the light.

CHAPTER TWENTY-ONE

Tripped Up

The woods soon gave way to more rocky crags they must either climb or go around, and since going around also meant the possibility of running into the ghostly crew, they opted to climb. Daphne's muscles ached when she dug in her feet and pulled herself up. At least the wounds on her leg and hip were scabbed and no longer bleeding. The wind lifted her ponytail and cooled her skin, moving through Brock's shirt and up her shorts.

"Stay close to the rock," Daphne warned. "We don't want to be spotted."

Once she reached the summit, she lay flat on her belly and looked over the edge. She gasped, because she saw something she had never seen before, even from the peak of Mount Diablo: a tower.

"That must be the naval tower," she told Brock once he had clamored up beside her, flat on his belly, too. "Cam told me about it on the way over. Real naval guards should be manning it."

"What do you mean 'real'? As opposed to unreal?"

She quickly explained what had happened with the girl in the valley and the interview with the supposed guards.

"This place really is screwed up," he said when she had finished her story.

"Do you think the real guards could help us?" she asked.

"I would think so. What do you think?"

"I say we go for it and get help."

They made their way over the rocky crags and back down toward another patch of lush trees. It was shady here, and the wind was gentler, and soon they came upon a path that led to a spring.

Daphne knelt by the water and submerged her face. She allowed some of the water to rush into her mouth. It tasted fresh and delicious.

"It worries me that we can't see the tower from down here," Brock said, "but this spring and this path must lead to it, don't you think?"

"Yeah. I would think so." Then she said, "I need water." The little taste from the spring hadn't been enough to quench her thirst.

He turned around so she could get the last bottle from the pack. Now that they could refill it with spring water, there was no reason to conserve it.

She gulped down half of it and then asked Brock if he wanted some. "It's so good," she said.

He drank the rest of it, and then bent over the stream and refilled the bottle.

Keeping their eyes out for signs of the others, they picked through the trees beneath the songs of birds and a new mossy smell, until they came upon a paved road running north and south. The south would lead them back to where they started, so they headed north. It was nice to have the sun and a sense of direction again.

The heat off the pavement made Daphne hot and sticky, and the sweat stung her sunburnt skin, but the smooth road was easier on her feet, even though it was uphill.

"I liked it better in the woods," Daphne said after a moment, not meaning to complain.

"I think I see something up ahead."

She craned her neck. "What?"

"A jeep."

"Not from the resort."

"I hope not. Let's get off the road."

They darted into the trees and crept toward the jeep for a better view of its passengers.

"Can you see anything?" Daphne asked.

"Not yet."

They trudged on, and soon Daphne saw the jeep and two men wearing white navy uniforms standing on the road talking.

"Thank God," she said. "Maybe they can help us."

She stepped onto the road ahead of Brock, but then she thought better of it. What if they were part of Hortense Gray's lot? Before she could retreat, one of the guards turned and spotted her.

"What are you two doing way out here? Lost?" the one with the glasses asked.

"Yes," Brock said, but at the same time, Daphne said, "No."

"Well, what is it? Are you lost or not?"

"Lost," Brock said. Then he added, "She thinks she knows where we are. You know how girls hate to stop and ask for directions."

The naval guards laughed along with Brock, and Daphne just smiled with as much charm as she could muster.

"So what brought you out this way?" The other guard, the blond, asked. "Hiking is prohibited in this area."

"We're trying to get back to Scorpion Anchorage so we can get off the island," Daphne said. "Can you give us a ride?"

"Sure, but that still doesn't explain why you're here."

"Oh, that would be so wonderful!" Daphne wanted to hug the naval guards. "We're so exhausted. We were guests of the resort until Dr. Gray's therapy got out of hand."

"Who's Dr. Gray?" the blond asked.

Daphne said, "She's the one conducting the experimental therapy at the resort on the other side of the island. But her games have gone too far. Can you take us now to Scorpion Anchorage?"

"Games?" the guard with the glasses asked. "What kind of games?"

"Let's just say one man's dead because of them."

"Wait a minute, Daphne. We don't know any of this for sure."

She gave Brock a dirty look. "Yes, we do."

"Hold on," the guard with glasses said. "Do you mean to say some-one's been killed?"

"I saw a body in the water. His first name was Pete. The tide washed him into a cave."

"What? Where?" the one with glasses asked.

She pointed. "Um, southwest of here near Bowen's Point."

"You don't sound lost," the blond said.

Daphne and Brock exchanged worried looks.

The guard with glasses asked, "Can you take us to where you saw the body?"

Daphne glanced again at Brock, and he shook his head and shrugged. "We really want to get off the island."

"Not if there's a dead body," the blond officer said. "We'll have to launch a formal investigation, which means shutting down all ports."

"Get in the jeep," the guard with glasses said.

The other guard climbed into the driver's side, radioing his alert.

The last thing she wanted was to be detained on the island. What if the naval officers took them back to the resort to question the others? And she still wasn't sure they weren't connected to Dr. Gray. Daphne glanced up at Brock with wide eyes, and, hoping he'd take her lead, she threw her water bottle at the guard standing next to her and ran across the road and into the woods on the other side. She glanced back to see Brock on her heels, but one of the guards wasn't far behind.

"Stop!" the guard ordered. "Stop, or I'll shoot!"

"This way!" Brock took her hand and pulled her to the side behind a large boulder and through a thicket.

Branches scraped against her flesh, but she ran at her top speed, keeping up with Brock's pace. Glancing back, she could no longer see the guard behind them. Then she heard a shot. A flock of blue birds lifted from the trees and took flight.

"Keep going," she said. "Let's keep running for as long as we can."

The sun was at high noon, so it was difficult to know for sure if she was still running east. They slowed to cut through another thicket and then found themselves on an open field of purple morning glory. How she wished she could lie down on the purple blanket of flowers and go to sleep.

"Hurry," she said. "To those rocks."

They turned to what she hoped was the north and headed for a formation of boulders the size of houses. They climbed a whole neighborhood block of those boulders, up and down, up and down, helping each other along as quickly as they could move, until the ocean became visible.

"Look at all those boats," Brock said.

There were at least fifty boats moving through the sea.

"Should we go for it?"

She studied the huge round rock toward Scorpion Anchorage to the east. She was exhausted and sore and didn't want to climb another thing as long as she lived.

"Let's go," she said.

She looked back to see three ghost girls and at least four men, one of them Stan, trailing behind them below.

"Hurry!" she cried.

"Daphne, wait!' Stan called. "Let us explain!"

"Leave us alone!" she shouted as she pulled herself up the massive rock.

Brock climbed beside her. "You okay?"

She nodded as they pulled themselves to the top of the headland, from which they could now see the pier at Scorpion Anchorage. The wind raged against them, as if it, too, wished to keep them on the island. Below were at least a hundred yards of rolling rock between them and the pier.

She looked back to see Stan and two other men reaching the top of the last boulder.

"Daphne! Wait! I have a gun!"

They hurried down the rolling, solid rock toward the pier as shots rang out. Daphne tried not to run in a straight line, to avoid being an easy target.

"This way!" she shouted to Brock. "Zigzag!"

She heard another shot, and she flinched, losing her footing, and though she reached out with her hands to break the fall, her left knee hit hard, taking most her weight.

"Ahh!"

"Daphne!" Brock knelt beside her. "You okay?"

She tried to stand but fell back. The knee was too tender. "It hurts. God it hurts." She gently touched the kneecap, feeling it swell beneath her fingertips. "I think it's broken." Tears brimmed in her eyes.

"No, Daph! I'm so sorry!" He swept her up in his arms and cradled her against his chest. "Does it hurt your knee to be bent like this?"

"It hurts no matter what. Are you sure you can carry me?"

He spoke as he ran for the pier. "You're light as a feather, silly."

He carried her down the rocks, and after a few minutes, though the pain in her knee was sharp, she closed her eyes and allowed herself to relax in his arms. She was tired and wanted to go home and would give anything to be back in her bed in San Antonio with a coke in one hand and a slice of pizza in the other and the television on *American Idol*. She leaned her cheek against Brock's chest and sighed. She was so sleepy.

"Mmm," she said.

"You okay?"

"Mm-hmm."

She opened her eyes as he reached the wooden pier.

"Over here!" Brock called. "Help! Over here!"

Shaded from the sun by Brock's body, she felt the cool breeze from the sea sweep over her, and once again she closed her eyes and imagined herself at home, safe with Brock.

She jolted awake at the sound of another person's voice.

"Lay her down in here," a man with white whiskers and a Hawaiian print shirt said.

Brock followed the man into the cabin of the boat.

"What's happening?" Daphne asked, still in Brock's arms. She wondered how long she'd been sleeping.

He set her down on a cot and fluffed the pillow behind her head. "Go back to sleep. The doc's getting ice for your knee. Everything's going to be alright." He covered her with a sheet.

The cold sensation on her sore knee woke her again.

"It's okay," Brock's smooth voice said. "Go back to sleep and rest. Good news. Your knee's not broken, only bruised, but the doc's going to give you something for the pain."

"What?" she half-opened her eyes in time to see the whiskered man stick a needle in her shoulder.

"It will make you feel better," the old man said.

"What is it?"

"Morphine," Brock said. "To help you rest."

"Morphine? Why?" she asked with alarm, but before she could ask more, she felt the room spin, and the need to close her eyes was overpowering. "Brock What's happening?"

She heard him chuckle as he tenderly kissed her cheek. Then she dropped down into peaceful oblivion.

CHAPTER TWENTY-TWO

Limuw

Daphne felt someone touching her, but she couldn't open her eyes. She tried to speak, and in her mind, she was saying, "Brock?" but her lips did not move. The pain in her knee was no longer acute, but dull, and vague, like an old dream. A dream. She heard the thumping of Kara's headboard. Should she get up? (What's she doing, jumping on the bed? Sit-ups? Dancing?) But Daphne lay there, unable to move. Too tired. Knee hurts. Thirsty.

The thumping grew louder, like a bass drum, and she felt herself being rubbed down and then lifted. A smell of musk and peppermint and perspiration wafted near her face. Someone whispered at her ear. What? What did you say?

She heard singing above her. Not birds. People. Daphne tried to open her eyes, but they felt weighted down. She could not move her lips.

"It's okay, Daph."

Who is that? Kara?

Now she was rising up. She blinked several times at the clear blue sky above her.

"Limuw has taken her life, and our prayers are to Hutash. Hutash agrees it is not yet time. She has given us a ritual to bring Limuw back to life."

What? She blinked, again and again, the light bright above her.

Applause. She turned her head toward the sound of vigorous clapping.

"It's okay, Daphne," a whisper came near her ear. A hooded figure in white.

Oh no. Daphne sat up. Her hand rushed to her head. No! Her head was bald! Slick as a bowling ball. "My hair," she whispered. Tears pricked her eyes.

Five hooded people in white knelt before her.

"Limuw was dead and now she is alive again. Welcome back to the land of the living." It was Larry's voice.

More applause.

Individual faces became recognizable to Daphne—Hortense Gray, Stan, Emma, Roger, Arturo Gomez, Lee Reynolds, Phillip, Mary Ellen, Kelly, and many others in the amphitheater, applauding her as she sat dumbfounded. Anger filled her heart. Where was Brock? What had they done with Brock?

Before she could demand an explanation, she was lifted in a stretcher from her perch on the altar by the five hooded people and carried into the canyon wall into a room alight with candles. "Dave? Vince? Let me go!" She tried to get free, but found her legs were bound. Somewhere stringed instruments played a slow lament.

"Stop!" she shouted. "Let me out of here!"

The five took her to the wall of the cavernous room and sat her on a bench of rock before stretching her arms out to either side and cuffing them into shackles. Draped with a white sheet, no clothes underneath, she screamed, "Oh, my crap! Why are you doing this?"

"It's not why, but what," Larry's voice sounded, clear and low through the room.

"Please! Please let me go!"

The hooded people backed away and left her alone in the room. The music stopped. Only the candlelight remained.

"Please!" she screamed again. "Hello? Where's Brock? Cam, I told you I didn't want this! How can you let this happen! Anyone there? Please!"

A hooded person appeared before her carrying a bucket. The person lowered the hood to reveal her identity.

"Mother?" Daphne blinked her eyes, sure she was hallucinating. "Is that really you? Mom! Help me!"

Her mother stepped forward. "You should have gotten out of bed that night you heard Joey in Kara's room."

Before Daphne could respond, her mother lifted the bucket and threw cold water all over her, face and all.

Daphne sputtered, having no free hands to wipe the water from her mouth and eyes. She blinked rapidly several times, the cold water mixing with her hot tears. Her own mother had thrown water at her. Her own mother was part of the torment. When she opened her eyes, Brock stood before her, also carrying a bucket.

"Brock? You were in on it all along?" Her mouth gaped.

"You shouldn't have hurt me." He, too, splashed the water, with more force than her mother, all over her body.

She spat and cried, "How can you do this to me? I thought I could trust you! I thought you loved me? I'll never trust you again!" This couldn't be happening. It must be a nightmare.

Brock returned the hood to his head and turned and walked away.

Now her father appeared in a white robe with the hood down and with a bucket in one hand.

"Dad, help me!"

"This is for Joey." He threw the water at her.

Even her father! The person who'd always loved her the most was willing to hurt her! So cruel! Tears fell down her cheeks.

One after another, she was assaulted with buckets of cold water, so frequently she had no time to clear her eyes to see who the offenders were.

"Please!" she cried again and again as more buckets of cold water deluged her.

After ten or more buckets of water had been thrown on her, Daphne heard the stringed instruments playing a ballad, and then a voice, Larry's, rang out. "You've been purified, purged of all wrong-doing, and are clean, pure as a newborn infant."

She sobbed, overcome with anger and shock and shame. She wanted to cover her face, but her hands were still stretched out like Jesus's had been on the cross.

Larry continued to sing about her purification, but she did not feel clean; she felt angry and betrayed.

"Now it's your turn, Limuw. It's your turn to inflict the punishment and to purify others."

The hooded people returned to unbind her wrists. Then she was led by the arms across the room where other people in white hoods sat on rock benches with their hands shackled. She fought to be free but was held in place. The hood on the first shackled person was lifted. It was her mother.

"Take this bucket of water," Larry instructed. "Hit her with it."

Daphne shook her head. "I can't!"

"I blamed you, didn't I?" her mother said, her brown eyes wide like they were that morning they had found Kara. "I made you feel Kara's death was your fault. Please! I'm the one who was in denial about Joey! It was my fault, not yours!" Her mother's lips trembled as tears slid down her cheeks. "Please! Do it!"

Daphne hesitated, but her mother's pleading eyes made her take up the bucket and throw the water on her—not hard, just on her legs. Larry gave her another bucket and insisted she hit her mother from head to toe. She did, feeling a surprising lightness in her feet. Her mother sputtered, her dark brown hair flattened against her head, appearing both tragic and comic. The morning they found Kara, her mother had said, "What? You heard and did nothing?" She had immediately apologized, but the words had caged Daphne's heart, and throwing the bucket of water into her mother's face had loosened that cage, maybe even freed the heart.

The hood was lifted from the second person shackled beside her mother. It was her father.

"Hit me with it," her father said. "I should have been there for you."

Again, Daphne hesitated. Her father had said no damaging words to her, but he hadn't comforted her either. He had checked out, become aloof, like a body without a soul.

"Do it, Daphne," her father said.

Daphne took the bucket and threw it at her father. The expression on his soaked face made her giggle. She felt on the verge of hysterics and surprisingly…light.

Larry unhooded the third person seated and shackled after her father. It was Brock.

"I lied to you, Daphne. Punish me."

Daphne felt no hesitation. "I trusted you!" She hurled the water at his face. Then she turned to Larry. "Can I do that again?"

He gave her a second bucket.

"Go for it," Brock said. "I deserve it."

Daphne threw the water on him before he had gotten his words out. "Yes you do!" But as he gagged and coughed up water and his contrite blue eyes sought her, she wanted to rush to him with a towel and clear the water from his face.

She was led to one more hooded person, and she could tell, even before Larry threw back the hood, that the now golden skin and wiry frame belonged to Cam.

"Some best friend!" she cried.

"I wanted to help you."

She dumped the bucket on him as tears poured from her cheeks. She heard him sputtering as she was then taken out of the cave and onto the empty stage of the amphitheater. Hortense Gray marched down the stadium-style seats toward her and the stage.

"Survivor's guilt is common, Daphne. Many people have taken their lives because they couldn't live with it. We've created a place where people who suffer from it and other ailments can be cleansed of their guilt—whether guilt is warranted or not—so they can re-embrace life. We have dozens of patients here every month going through similar trials as you. A boy not much older than you arrived today who killed a two-year-old when he was driving under the influence of alcohol.

"You may be angry for a while about what we've done here. Most people are. They're especially upset by the loss of their hair. But we have found this therapy provides the dramatic impetus necessary for recovery."

"You're full of it!" Daphne shouted, the anger back in her throat. "You should be arrested and thrown in prison for what you've put me through. You should be the one in shackles. Along with my parents! Where are they anyway? Let me pour buckets of cold water on you, Dr. Gray! You murderer! What about Pete?"

"Believe it or not, you'll have your chance to judge me, but first, you have to go through the waiting period."

"Do you deny Pete's dead because of you?"

Just then another hooded person stepped forward and removed his hood. It was Pete. He was alive.

Daphne's mouth gaped. "How can that be? I saw him with my own eyes."

"Stan and I were hanging out at the pier waiting for you," Pete said. "I was tethered to it, so I could float there long enough for you to see me. Then, when it was clear you recognized me, Stan, who was diving with an oxygen tank and everything, cut me loose. He met me in the sea cave where we hung out till we thought you were gone."

"That's so cruel! Why did you do it? What was the point?"

Hortense stepped closer. "We wanted you to fear for your life. We've had actors, many who have been through the program…"

"Like me," Pete interrupted. "Everything I told you about my family was true. I tried to take my life. This place has changed me."

"And me," Stan said. "I really am an anthropologist. I do study the Chumash ruins and write papers. I was also married once, like I said. I hit the ground hard when my wife left. This place helped me see how much I want to live. So, I live here now. I write my papers and help this place at the same time."

"But what about that gash on your head, when we were on the haunted side of the island."

"Self-inflicted." Stan shrugged. "Not a big deal if it meant saving a life."

Daphne jerked her head back. "Why your face? Now you'll have a scar. If you were going to do something so stupid, you should have done it on your arm or leg where you could hide it."

As Daphne spoke those last few words, she recalled the scars on Hortense Gray's arm and gasped. She sought her eyes for confirmation, but the doctor briefly met her gaze and looked away.

Had Hortense Gray inflicted those scars on herself for the sake of her therapeutic exercises? And was it something she had learned from her father?

Hortense added, "We have many benefactors, in addition to Arturo Gomez, who help fund this program, many who suffer from depression and have gone through earlier programs not nearly as refined as what we have now. You met Mary Ellen Jones—she's another one. Currently, our clients pay quite a sum of money. But one day we hope to make this program accessible to as many as possible."

Daphne closed her eyes and sighed. "It's a mean trick." She fought back more tears. "I feel so betrayed, by all of you."

"That's why you must now go through the waiting period," Hortense said.

"The what?"

"You and your parents will remain here for another week to enjoy the beauty of your surroundings. Think about you're experience. Then, you'll go home until one day, when you're finally ready, when your hair has grown in, you'll return to discuss your progress."

"Yeah right! I'm never coming to this place again! Where are my parents? I want them to take me home now!"

"Keep in mind your parents and Brock and Cameron love you so much they put you through a rigorous program as a last resort to save you from yourself. No matter how angry you feel at the moment, you must see the good the program's already done you."

Tears fell down her cheeks and she could think of nothing to say, for she *had* worked through a lot of her feelings while on the island, and hadn't she chosen to live? Cam had said it sometimes takes a dramatic and painful experience to help you let go of the past. Was she now free to let go of the past?

"That silver bracelet around your wrist is given to every participant," Dr. Gray said. "The chain symbolizes the past that holds us back, what you need to break free from; but it also symbolizes the bonds that tie us all together. We try to help you transform the former into the latter." Then she said, "Daphne, the past is immutable."

"What does that mean?"

"Unchangeable. You can't change the past. You can only learn to live with it."

Daphne looked at the bracelet, and, although she thought it was pretty, she wanted to rip it from her wrist. She glared back at Hortense and said nothing, realizing she'd seen the same bracelet on Cam's wrist.

Stan came closer, revealing something beneath his robe: the island fox. "Someone wants to say hi." He walked up to Daphne and gingerly passed the fox over to her.

She couldn't believe it. Relief swept over her. The fox had lived! It was warm and soft as it nestled its nose into the crook of her arm. "It's not hurt?"

"Nope. Good as new, kiddo. His tail was bruised, but he's fine now."

Like a house cat, the fox rubbed his head against the underside of her palm. She stroked him and smiled.

"What's his name?"

"Mini-me."

"Mini-me," she repeated. Peace washed over her as she cradled the fox and tears fled from her eyes. "I'm sorry I hurt you," she said to Mini-me. "It wasn't your fault." As she hugged the fox, she felt like she was hugging herself.

<u>CHAPTER TWENTY-THREE</u>

A Final Shock

As frightened as Daphne was to be alone in her room in Unit One, she refused to move into another unit to accommodate her and her parents. She had demanded that they return her home immediately, but they said the therapy required they all stay as a family for another few days.

She was sick and tired of what the therapy required.

Besides, Joey was still living in his facility back in Houston and Kara was dead. Her parents could call them a family all they wanted, and it wouldn't make it so. And although throwing the buckets of water on her parents and Brock and Cam *had* felt good, it hadn't meant she would ever forgive them.

Exhausted, she took a warm shower, scrubbing all the oil from her skin. After toweling herself dry, she stood before the mirror, horrified again by her hairless body. She looked inhuman—more like a giant tadpole. Tears stung her eyes as she turned away and climbed into sweats and a hoodie, covering her bald head with the hood.

She was tempted to stay in the bathroom because of the cameras, but she decided she didn't care, since all she wanted to do was crawl into bed and sleep. As she lay beneath the covers and closed her eyes, the events of the past several days ran over and over in her mind, like a film on a loop. She felt like such a fool. They had played her, and she had let them. She clenched her fists and rolled over to her side, and then punched a fist into her pillow and fought the urge to scream. She couldn't sleep. Would probably never be able to sleep again.

She threw off the covers and slipped on her shoes. She needed air.

It was dark by this time, and although a basket of food had been waiting for her in her room, she hadn't eaten since she and Brock had shared their snack in the woods. That seemed like such a long time ago. Nevertheless, she had no appetite. Her entire body felt numb and shaky.

Though the deck area in the center of the resort was dark, the lights from inside the pool cast a glow onto two people sitting on loungers. Gregory Gray and Emma leaned close together, maybe even kissing. She crept past and headed for the beach.

The wind chilled her when she reached the top of the steps, which were lit by tall lamps, so anyone who looked up would see her standing there. But with her hood pulled low over her eyes, she might not be recognized. Unlike the wooden steps, the beach was covered by shadows, and the hill of poppies to her left and the bluffs to her right were shrouded in darkness. But the light from the moon was enough to see that there were people below near the shore. Daphne stole down a few of the steps to get a better look.

At first, they were huddled together, and she couldn't make out much about them except that they all wore black. But then one of them shot a fist into the air and screeched, "Wooh hoo!" The huddle then broke up in a whirl of laughter and hand clapping, and before Daphne could make out individual faces, one of them looked up, noticed her, and waved. The face wasn't familiar and looked pale in the moonlight. Then the group ran toward the steps below, heading straight up for Daphne, who stood there, frozen, unsure whether to wait for them or to run.

As they got closer, she noticed the white powder covering their bodies and black clothes. They had the same blue lips and red goo dripping from their eyes and mouths as the ghost girl and company who came to Daphne's room her first night at the Purgatorium. They clamored up the stairs toward her, laughing and smiling, but this made them seem even creepier than when they told her with their somber faces that she was one of the dead. Just as Daphne was about to turn and run back to her unit, she recognized one of the leaders. It was Cam.

He took her hand as the other ghosts ran past her and said, "Come with us."

"What's happening?" she asked.

"We're going to haunt the new arrivals. Come on. You'll get a kick out of this."

As the others passed by her, she recognized rowdy Dave, quiet Vince, Bridget, and Stan.

"Welcome, kiddo," Stan said before running ahead of her after Bridget.

Cam held tight to her hand as they ran down the steps behind the others, reentering the resort proper. Gregory and Emma gave a friendly wave to the mob of the six of them as they hurried past the pool, down the sidewalk, to one of the other units.

Then Cam pulled Daphne around the side of the building behind a shrub. "Since you're not in costume, you hang back here and watch through the window. We'll try to get them out of the unit so you can get a better view."

"Better view of what?"

"Just don't let yourself be seen. It would ruin everything."

Daphne crouched behind the shrub and peered through the window. The lights were off, so she could see nothing but the vague outline of furniture in the dim moonlight. Then, from the bed, she heard voices.

"Give it a while. These things take time."

It was her father's voice!

"You don't think it was a mistake?" her mother asked. "Mary Ann Turner swore by this place, but that performance this evening, well, that was not what I was expecting."

"Nor I, but I thought we decided this was our last hope. And Dr. Gray's track record is impressive."

"I know. You're right."

There was a pounding on their front door.

Her mother asked, "Do you think that's Daphne?"

"Who else?" her father said, climbing out of the bed.

Daphne felt the urge to warn her father, to shout, "It's not me! Don't answer it!" but another part of her was glad he would get a dose of his own medicine. A soft giggle escaped her lips.

Her father crossed the room to the door.

Daphne covered her smiling mouth.

Her father opened the door. "Daph?" The light from the porch illuminated him on the stoop in his striped pajamas.

"Trick or treat!" Dave growled before lifting his gun and spraying Daphne's father with white powder.

"Ahh!" her father shouted with his hands waving in the air.

Before he could close the door, a trio of ghosts entered the room and stood over her mother, where she lay in the bed. They pointed their guns at her and asked, "Are you one of the living or the dead?"

"What?" her father moved between them and her mother. "What's going on here?"

"You're one of the dead, Sharon Janus!" Bridget shouted as they all three shot both of Daphne's parents with powder. Then the trio of ghosts fled from the room.

But Daphne's father ran out after them. "What the hell is going on?"

Daphne stepped from the shrub and peered around the building to get a better view.

Cam and the rest of the group circled her father and chanted, "You're one of the dead. You're one of the dead. You're one of the dead," before her father broke their ring and scrambled back into the room.

Daphne returned to the window to see him close and lock the door, and then, just as Daphne had done her first night on the island, he slid one of the upholstered chairs in front of the door.

Daphne's mother had climbed from the bed and was trembling in the corner of the room. Daphne could barely see her, for she was in shadows, but occasionally her hands would fly to her face or back down to her stomach, and their trembling was unmistakable.

"I don't understand," Sharon said when her husband turned on the light and ran to her.

"Are you okay?"

"Of course. It's only talcum powder. But what was that all about?"

"I intend to find out." Her father grabbed the phone on the bedside table and dialed.

Apparently no one answered on the other end, for he all but screamed into the phone, "Dr. Gray, I would appreciate it if you would call me as soon as possible. This is not at all what we signed up for." Then he slammed the phone back onto its cradle.

Sharon brought Joe a towel from the bathroom and helped him wipe off the powder, as she had already done to her own face and arms.

"It doesn't come off all that well," Sharon said. "But it's only powder. The skin will absorb it, unless you want to take a shower."

"That can wait until morning," he said. "Let's turn on the TV and try to go to bed. Hopefully this nonsense is over."

"I think we should leave tomorrow, don't you?" Sharon said as she climbed beneath the covers. "Mary Ann swears by this doctor. Cam thinks she hung the moon. And her track record and credentials are impressive, as you said. But this is too strange for my tastes."

"Absolutely." Joe turned off the lamp and climbed beside her where the light from the television bathed them in a purplish hue.

"Do you think they did that to Daphne?" her father asked after a while.

"I hope not," Sharon replied.

Daphne shook her head thinking, *You have no idea.*

Just then, Cam took her hand and put his finger to his lips. She followed him from her parents' unit back toward the beach. When they were a safe distance away from her parents' room, as they climbed the steps of the boardwalk, he asked her, "What did you think?"

"It was hilarious. I could barely hold back my laughter."

"I know, right? Your dad was hilarious!"

They continued down to the beach out of the light of the boardwalk to where the pale moon cast a subtle glow on the sea.

"Did you hear what my mom said?" Daphne asked. "She wondered if y'all had done that to me. If only she knew!"

They walked along the sand, arm in arm. In spite of her excitement, Daphne still hadn't decided whether she could forgive Cam, but for now, she basked in the moment.

"She's about to find out," Cam said.

"What do you mean?" Daphne stopped in her tracks and studied Cam's face.

"You enjoyed the game with the ghosts, right?"

"Yeah?"

"Good. Then maybe you'd like to help us with your parents' games. And Brock's too."

"What do you mean?"

"They don't know it, but they're going to get therapy, too," Cam explained.

Daphne's mouth dropped open. "You mean…therapy like mine?"

"Yeah, but based on their profiles, not yours."

"Their profiles?" She waited for Cam's explanation.

"Their fears."

"Are you telling me that Brock and my parents are about to get the crap scared out of them, and I get to help?"

Even behind the white powder and red goo, she could see Cam smile. "That's exactly what I'm telling you."

A thrill moved through Daphne. She couldn't wait to start the new games.

As they turned back toward the boardwalk, a lone figure stood there above them. Beneath the bright lights, Daphne could see it was Hortense Gray. The doctor raised a hand, more like a "Heil, Hitler" than a wave. Daphne and Cam lifted their hands and waved. Although she still wasn't sure how she felt about the doctor's strange therapy, Daphne had to admit she had never felt more alive than she did right at that moment.

THE END

Thank you for reading my story. If you enjoyed it, please consider leaving a review. Reviews help other readers to find my books, which helps me.

Please enjoy this excerpt from the next book, *Gray's Domain*.

CHAPTER ONE

Ghosts

Daphne Janus left her unit at Santa Cruz Island Resort, crept past the abandoned pool glowing in the darkness, and made her way down the sidewalk beyond the other cabanas. The wind blew heavily tonight, and she pulled the hoodie further down over her eyes—not because it was cold out, but because she did not want her bald head exposed. She stifled a giggle as she reached Brock's unit and knocked on the door.

The door opened, and there was Brock, in a white t-shirt and boxers and with mussed up hair and puffy eyes, looking as sexy as ever. "Daph?"

"I'm scared. Can I come in?"

He blinked. "Of course."

He opened the door wider, and she slipped by, trying not to laugh.

"I'm surprised you're talking to me." He ran a hand through his dark, unruly hair, which only further reminded her that her own was gone.

But enough self-pity. It angered her that he looked so hot with bed-head and sleepy blue eyes. She fought the urge to kiss him.

"I heard strange noises outside my room," she lied. "Can I sleep here tonight?"

He placed his hand over his heart, like he was about to recite *The Pledge of Allegiance.* "Does this mean you forgive me?"

Absolutely not, she thought. "I think so."

He stepped closer and touched his lips to hers. His lips were soft and thick and felt good, but the memory of what he'd done to her over the past couple of days, making her believe he was on her side, brought the clarity she needed to resist. She bit down hard on his bottom lip.

"Ow!" He flinched back, hands rushing to his mouth. "I guess I deserved that."

And so much more, she thought. *But don't worry. Payback is coming.*

"I'm sorry." She sat on the edge of the bed and stared at her lap. "I have mixed feelings about everything. I know you were only trying to help, but…"

He sat beside her, not quite touching her, and licked the blood from his lip. "I know." Without looking at her, he said, "The whole time I was doing it, I wasn't sure. Dr. Gray made it seem right."

She rubbed her thighs, suddenly chilled beneath her sweats. Brock had meant her no harm. He had wanted to help her. She was wrong to deceive him back. But wasn't *she* helping *him* now? It was revenge, but it was also therapy. "I just wish I could know for sure how much of it was real."

He lifted her chin and gazed into her eyes. "Everything about how I feel—all of that was real. Please say you believe me. It'll kill me if you don't."

Payback didn't look so good anymore. "Oh, Brock."

He kissed her again, taking her in his arms. His mouth tasted like mint with a hint of blood, and his hair smelled clean and musky. The muscles in his chest and shoulders enveloped her, exciting her. He pressed her down on the bed as tears sprang to her eyes. She clutched the hood to keep it from revealing her head. That's all it took—the memory of her hair being shaved while he did nothing to stop it—to call up her anger.

He reached his hand to her bare scalp, but she pulled away.

"Don't," she said.

"You're still beautiful, you know."

"I don't feel beautiful." She sat up on the edge of the bed.

He sat up beside her, not quite touching her again. "But do you think this place helped you?"

As mad as she was at all of them for tricking her in such a cruel way—making her think she was in danger, terrifying her into running for her life—she had to admit she no longer felt like the pitiful girl she was a week ago. She wasn't sure, though, if her feelings of self-loathing and guilt hadn't simply been replaced by a need for revenge. Once she put her parents and Brock through the same terrifying torture as they had put her, would the self-loathing return?

"I think so," she finally said.

"It'll probably take time to know for sure."

She didn't like how nice he was being to her.

He covered her hand with his. "I want to be there for you, Daph. Please don't shut me out again."

Then a loud knock on the door made her jump. The ghosts, she thought.

"Who else would be knocking this late?" Brock crossed the room to the door.

She shrugged and shook her head, the thrill of the game making her tremble with excitement. She felt on the verge of hysteria as she waited for him to open the door.

He peered through one of the front windows. "I can't tell who's there, but it looks like a group of kids."

The door burst open. Brock moved between the intruders and Daphne. Five of them stood in the doorway with their faces and clothes covered in white powder. Red goo dripped from red eyes and blue lips.

"What's going on?" Brock held his arms out like a shield between the ghosts and Daphne.

"Are you one of the living or the dead?" a ghost boy, probably Dave, asked in a low growl.

"What the hell? Get out! Do you know what time it is?" Brock charged them, but before he reached them, a turbo-sized water gun sprayed white powder all over him. He rushed his hands to his face, shouting obscenities.

Daphne jumped from the bed, eager to play along. That's when a pale hand wrapped itself around her wrist and dragged her from the room.

"Come with us," one of the ghosts, whom she now recognized as Cam, whispered quickly at her ear. "Pretend we're abducting you."

He had his black hood pulled low over his eyes, making him unrecognizable. Her parents, whom he had helped torment about an hour ago, hadn't recognized Cam either. She had watched from behind a shrub through the window of their unit as the ghosts played their mischief on her parents. Another giggle escaped her throat as she recalled the high she had felt then—the same high she felt now.

Her cheeks stretched wide. "Love it."

"Let's make a run for it," he whispered. "The others will hold him back."

She and Cam sprinted past the pool toward the boardwalk. At this late hour, well after midnight, no one else roamed the sidewalks of the resort. Even Gregory and Emma had left the poolside where they had been making out earlier in the evening. The place felt abandoned. Only a few lights on the third floor of the main building showed signs of life.

"Daphne?" Brock cried from the room.

"We're taking her with us!" one of the ghosts—Bridget—said as Daphne raced away.

"Daphne!" Brock called again.

When Daphne and Cam reached the boardwalk, Daphne shouted at the top of her lungs, not sure if he would hear her, "Brock! Help! These people are crazy!"

She smiled gleefully and followed Cam, her heart pumping as she skipped down the wooden steps to the sand, where the moonlight illuminated the sea.

"Lie down here on the beach while the rest of us hide in the shadows," Cam instructed. "We'll ambush the both of you. You play the terrified victim, 'kay?"

"Got it."

He squeezed her hand. "You okay?"

She nodded, not sure what he meant. Physically, she felt great. And at the moment, she felt exuberant, never better.

He kissed her cheek and dashed away.

Two other ghosts joined Cam in the shadows of the bluffs as Daphne lay on her back on the cool sand by the shore. The moon was waning but still nearly full, and the stars were brilliant in a cloudless sky. The breeze off the sea chilled her.

Turning toward the boardwalk, she screamed in the otherwise quiet night, "Brock! Help me!"

Brock soon appeared on the top of the boardwalk, followed by the last two ghosts—Stan and Dave—who must have held him back.

Again, she screamed, "Brock! I'm down here!"

He rushed down the steps and knelt at her side.

"What happened? Are you okay?"

Before she could answer, all five ghosts surrounded them, chanting, "You are not living! You are the dead! You are not living! You are the dead!"

Brock shoved the actors down on the sand, scooped Daphne into his arms, and raced up the wooden steps toward the resort. She could feel his heart hammering in his chest against her, his breath pumping hard as it was sucked in and out. A thrill moved through her. Even though she knew this was all an act, it was nevertheless titillating. At the top of the steps, Brock looked back at the ghosts, who were no longer following them but had disappeared in the shadows.

"This is bullshit," he said, along with a few other choice words. "Are you okay? Can you walk?"

"I think so."

He set her on her feet and then pressed his hands to his knees, trying to catch his breath.

"Thanks for coming to my rescue." She tried to sound spooked.

"What the hell just happened?" he asked her as he led her back to his room, holding tightly to her hand. "Did they hurt you?"

"No. They just scared me, that's all." She dusted sand from her bottom. "You don't think they were real ghosts, do you?"

"Of course not, but I thought the games were over. I've had enough."

She wanted to say, *So it's not so fun being on the other side*, but she held her tongue because, for one thing, she couldn't let him know how she really felt, and, for another, because she knew from experience, that despite his anger, a part of him had found the experience as thrilling as she.

The door to his room was ajar, so he went in first, turned on more lights, and checked around before motioning Daphne inside. She avoided his eyes, finding it hard not to laugh. She wanted to jump up and down and exhibit the feelings of excitement that were building up inside her, but she pretended to be frightened and shaken by the experience. Brock locked the door and pulled one of the chairs against it as she and her parents had both done before him, while she covered her face with her hands and tried to get a grip on her feelings. All she could think was how much she couldn't wait for the next game to begin.

A half hour later, after she and Brock had taken turns in the shower, she lay in clean borrowed clothes in Brock's arms biting her lips to keep from giggling. She could only imagine how much fun the next few days would be. She wondered what Hortense had in store for Brock and her parents. Would they get stuck in a dark elevator like she had with Stan?

Would their kayak group get trapped with Hairy Larry in a sea cave by the tide? Would they be bucked off their horses during their trail ride with Kelly and get lost on the haunted side of the island?

This last thought upset her. Although she wanted to frighten her parents and Brock, she didn't want them to get hurt. She could have been killed falling off of the horse. Ironically, that was what she had hoped for when she had agreed to come with Cam to this island. She'd wanted to die. It seemed like such a long time ago. She recalled kneeling in the stream in Central Valley after escaping from Stan and Larry, and then lying on her back, like the woman in the painting in Hortense's office. The thought of taking her life now seemed stupid.

She still regretted not getting up that night her brother went to her sister's room, and in his sickness, attempted to strangle a demon from their sister's body. She still believed she might have changed the out-come of that terrible moment if she had gone into Kara's room when she was awakened by the thumping sound, but she now understood she hadn't caused Kara's death. She wasn't responsible. Her brother, Joey, was sick. Hortense Gray's strange therapeutic games had forced her to face the truth: she was helpless against the past. It was immutable—the word Hortense had used, meaning unchangeable. Taking her life would solve nothing.

If she had her poetry journal, she would write:

Today is another day

And tomorrow, too;

And though I miss your sweet voice

You're in everything I do.

She wanted her parents and Brock to benefit from Hortense Gray's therapy, but she wouldn't allow their lives to be risked in the same way. As she lay there composing poetry and listening to Brock's steady breathing beside her, she decided she would visit Hortense in the morn-ing and make sure no rough play was part of the games.

First she'd have to convince her parents and Brock to stay. After their encounter with the ghosts, they sounded determined to leave. Daphne couldn't let that happen. She had way too much to look forward to in the form of their torment to let them leave now.

In the morning, Daphne awoke before Brock. She snuck out to take another shower and dress in her room. She put on the scarf her mother had brought, and the fact that her mother had known to bring it renewed her anger and need for revenge. She decided to give her parents a call and ask them to meet her for breakfast. She used her friendliest voice. Her father sounded shocked but agreed.

Up in the third-floor banquet hall, she spotted her parents sitting together at a table by themselves, avoiding eye contact with the other people, who were going back and forth from the breakfast buffet to their seats. Both her parents wore khaki shorts and light-colored button-down shirts. Her mother wore her frosted hair pulled back in the thick brown headband that had become her staple accessory. She suddenly looked small and fragile sitting there next to Daphne's father. Daphne also spotted Cam, Emma, Gregory, Pete, and Stan sitting with Hortense, fawning over the doctor like they all had school-girl crushes, all wearing silver bracelets exactly like the one on Daphne's wrist. They gave Daphne friendly waves, and she nodded to them in return, still feeling ambivalent about their roles in her torment. Brock was nowhere in sight. She frowned and worried she should have called him and told him she'd meet him here, too.

Her parents looked up at her when she approached their table.

"Can I sit with you?" she asked.

"Of course," her mother said, her brows in a v. "You don't have to ask."

She noticed they had waited for her before making their plates. "Let's go get some grub, then."

As they filled their plates with eggs, hash browns, fruit, and muffins, her father warned her that they planned to leave as soon as possible.

"But this place is helping me," Daphne said, which wasn't a lie. "I want to finish the therapy."

Her parents exchanged looks of surprise, and when they returned to their table to eat, her father said, "Well, that's good to hear, Daph. An absolute relief."

Daphne noticed tears brimming in his eyes, and she flooded with guilt over what she planned to do to them.

"We'll stay as planned, then," her mother said, pulling the scarf a little further down on Daphne's head.

Daphne flinched from her mother's touch, causing her mother to frown and look away, down at her plate.

"I'm sorry," Daphne muttered. She hadn't realized how angry she still felt toward her mother. She had so many feelings bottled inside of her, and for some reason, most of the negative ones were brought on by her mother.

Maybe it was because she had said those words that continued to haunt Daphne: "You mean you heard and did nothing?"

Daphne had wanted to die then. She had wanted to curl up in a ball and die.

The past is immutable, she reminded herself as she twirled the silver bracelet on her wrist. *We can only learn to live with it.*

As they ate, she listened to her parents recount what had happened the night before with the ghosts. Daphne fought hard not to smile, especially at her mother's exaggerations—there were ten or twenty? They were all over six feet tall? Before they had finished eating, though, Hortense appeared beside their table, looming over Daphne like an evil spirit. *No, like Prospero.*

"I need to speak with you privately in my office," she said to Daphne. "Please come by when you're finished." Then she looked at Daphne's parents, gave them a curt nod, and left the dining hall.

EVA POHLER

Eva Pohler is a *USA Today* bestselling author of over thirty novels in multiple genres, including mysteries, thrillers, and young adult paranormal romance based on Greek mythology. Her books have been described as "addictive" and "sure to thrill"—*Kirkus Reviews*.

To learn more about Eva and her books, and to sign up to hear about new releases, and sales, please visit her website at www.evapohler.com.